To everyone who struggles with difficult situations.
There is always hope.

Prologue

The judge's stern eyes glared at Ryan. "You've been before this court many times, Ryan Jenkins," he said. "And nothing has changed."

Ryan looked up at the judge, not saying a word. The judge looked like a long-nosed rat with beady eyes. His mouth seemed to twitch underneath his stringy moustache.

"You've been in and out of juvenile detention, mostly for stealing cars. Your court record includes break and enter charges."

"You've broken the rules and had fights while in custody, plus an escape. The list goes on and on. Now another car theft. Nothing the court has given you has stopped you from breaking the law. So I'm trying something different."

Ryan's gut churned. His shoulders stiffened, bracing for what would come next.

"I believe you can change," the judge said at last. "The assessment report says you're a smart seventeen-year-old. Use what you have to figure out your life. Make it work."

"Yes, Your Honour."

"This time I'm giving you a four-month CSO — a conditional sentencing order."

Ryan's brow wrinkled.

"It means the police are watching you. You need to do the community work I give you and go to school. Stay away from the guys who got you in trouble with the law. Don't even think about breaking the eight-o'clock curfew or breaching the order by leaving the province."

Ryan's shoulders relaxed. "No juvie time," he said under his breath.

The judge's face looked grim. "Don't think this will be easy. It won't. Breach just one of those conditions and it's back to juvenile detention. Understand?"

"Yes, Your Honour."

The gavel hit hard. The sound bounced through Ryan's brain. He turned and left the courtroom.

As he walked down the courthouse steps, he muttered, "Never again. I'll never go back to juvie. I'll finish the CSO and be done with it. Nothing will stop me."

Chapter 1

Trapped

Ryan stared out the apartment window, wishing he could escape. A month had crawled by since the judge had given him the CSO. He felt trapped by the eight-o'clock curfew. Every night he had to stay in an empty apartment while his dad was at the bar getting drunk.

Enough, Ryan decided. He grabbed his jacket, opened the apartment door, and headed downstairs to the ground floor. Easing open the main door, he looked around for the cops. It was after curfew. He took a deep breath and stepped out onto the main street of Mill Town. The street lights were dim in the gloom of the evening. The smell of the pulp mill hung heavy in the air.

Ryan's fists tightened, making the letters tattooed on the knuckles of his right hand stand out. He walked onward, his ragged runners hitting the sidewalk with firm steps.

A Nissan GT-R zipped past. Rap music blared from its open windows. Ryan saw the teen driver at the wheel. The driver's buddy, next to him, yelled rap lyrics at the top of his lungs. The car swerved down the street. *Probably boosted*, Ryan thought. He was glad it wasn't Dan Main and his flunky Connor Cog — guys he'd been sent to juvie with for stealing cars. If he never saw that jerk Dan again, it would be too soon.

Ryan kicked a stone on the road. It zinged against a garbage can at the side of an apartment building. A cat hissed in the night. Ryan turned right onto a tree-lined street.

Most of the houses and apartments were in darkness. Some were lit by the flickering light of a TV. Ryan headed up the street, rounded the corner, and walked another block. Lights were on in two houses. A lady standing in a window across the street nodded at him as he walked by. Surprised that someone was being friendly, he waved back.

The beam of a flashlight shone in the dark interior of the house across the street. It was three doors up from where Ryan stood. The light bounced this way and that — searching.

Ryan's eyes widened. *I've got to get out of here. I'm not going to get blamed for a B and E*, he thought.

An alarm blared in the night. The front door banged open.

Ryan froze.

Connor Cog bolted from the house.

"You set off the alarm," bellowed a short, stocky teen who came sprinting after Connor. Ryan scowled. It was Dan.

Connor lumbered across the lawn. He was bigger than Dan but slower. Dan caught up to him and punched him in the back. Connor fell on the ground. Dan kept pounding him.

Ryan groaned. Connor was getting the worst of it. He wished Connor would turn on Dan and beat him up. Ryan knew Dan was like the dregs at the bottom of a beer can — gritty and bitter.

Lights flicked on in the house next door. A man threw open a window. "What's going on out there?" he yelled. "I'm calling the cops."

Dan and Connor stopped fighting and ran.

"Crap," said Ryan. His eyes darted about the neighbourhood for an exit. He ran toward the shadows of a house next to a laneway. Ryan flattened his body against a wall and waited. He had a clear view of the action on the street.

"What the hell, Dan? Can't you stay out of my freaking life?" Ryan muttered, as he watched Dan run past the house where the lady was watching in the window.

Connor crossed farther down the road and hid behind a pile of wood at the end of a driveway. The wood was lit by a nearby street light.

Dumbass, Ryan thought. *The cops will get him for sure.* A small pile of wood couldn't hide Connor's large frame.

Sirens screamed in the night. Two cop cars came down the street from opposite directions. The red and blue lights lit up the neighbourhood.

"Shit," Ryan said. He moved a bit farther down the lane, into a deeper shadow. He pulled the beak of his baseball cap down closer to his brow to hide his face.

Wheels screeched as the cop cars came to a halt. A cop jumped out, yelling, "Police. Stop!"

Two cops ran after Dan. One spotted Connor in the woodpile. A fourth shone his flashlight across the street. Ryan edged farther down the lane.

The cop's flashlight shone on Ryan. "Police! Stay where you are."

Ryan ran down the lane searching for any possible escape.

The cop raced after him. "Stop. Police! There's nowhere for you to go."

Ryan turned right and ran across a backyard. A leashed Rottweiler snarled, showing its white fangs. Ryan's heart pounded. He leapt the rear fence and sprinted into the woods behind the row of houses. He hoped the cop was out of shape.

Maybe I can lose him in the forest, Ryan thought.

"Police. We want to question you," wheezed the cop.

Ryan zigzagged between the fir trees. Their branches brushed his jacket and face. Sweat ran down his back. He heard the cop running somewhere behind him. The sound of the cop's footsteps stopped. The light from his flashlight played left, then right. Ryan darted deeper into the woods. When he felt safe, he bent over to catch his breath.

Idiot, damn idiot, I should have stayed home, he thought. *Now I'm in shit again.*

Chapter 2

Run

Ryan listened to make sure the cop had given up the chase. There were no snapping twigs, no footsteps. Just silence among the trees.

He wondered if the cop got a good look at his face. Was it enough to identify him? A shiver ran down his back.

If the cop saw me, it's back to juvie for breaking curfew, Ryan thought. *With my luck, I'll probably get extra time for a B and E I didn't commit.*

He was sure no one would believe him. No one ever did.

"What the hell do I do now?" he mumbled. "Wait it out and see what happens? Or get as far away as possible?"

He needed to think. It was time to head home. His dad might have passed out on the couch by now. Better still: the old man might stay out all night. Ryan started walking.

A half hour later, Ryan eased open the door to his dad's apartment. He listened for the sound of snoring, but the place was as quiet as a graveyard. Flicking on the lights, he walked to his bedroom closet and stuffed his clothes into a duffel bag. A framed picture of his sister was nailed to the inside of the closet door. Ryan carefully removed it and flipped it over. He opened the back of the frame and grabbed the money he'd hidden inside. It was his earnings from fighting fires while on a forestry course in juvie. He stuffed the money into his worn wallet, fixed the frame, and put the picture carefully in the duffel's side pocket. Ryan took off the jacket and gloves he was wearing and packed them into the bag.

He dropped the duffel next to the ragged couch. Then he noticed the used toothpicks scattered on the living room floor. Ryan hated the old man's habit of picking his teeth. He picked at his teeth like he picked at everything and everyone.

Ryan glanced at his cheap watch. It was one in the morning. If the old man hadn't come home by now, he wouldn't be back until daylight. Ryan looked at the couch. He was exhausted. A few winks of sleep wouldn't hurt. Besides, where would he go if he left at this hour? He flopped on the couch. His eyes closed. In an instant, he was asleep, dreaming the same old dreams.

He was thirteen again. His first time in juvie — sweating scared. Doors clanged, and then he was in the gym, being pushed and punched by other teens. An alarm blared. Now he was spread-eagled against a wall, being searched.

A door banged. Ryan's eyes shot open. He was in his dad's apartment. He squinted at the sunlight streaming through the window.

His dad staggered into the living room, his shirt half out of his grimy pants. He glared at Ryan. "You no good, lazy piece of shit," he yelled. "You're like a leech sucking me dry. I've got no job, no wife, nothing. You're the cause of every rotten thing that's happened to me. Your mother left me 'cause you're such a lousy kid."

"No way," Ryan yelled back. "She left because of you."

"Get the hell out my life!" his dad bellowed. "You'll land back in juvie for sure. And when you're eighteen in January, it will be adult prison for you, mister. The cops will get you."

"Maybe they'll come and take you away instead," Ryan shouted.

"Don't you talk to me that way. Get the hell out. I've a good mind to beat the tar out of you." He staggered toward Ryan.

Ryan grabbed the duffel bag, dodged his dad's fists, and ran out the open door.

"Go, you piece of crap," his old man called after him. "I wish I'd never seen your face."

The old man continued to yell as Ryan ran down the stairs and out of the building. He burst onto a street lit by the early morning sun.

After a block of running, Ryan slowed down. He caught his breath and scanned the street. His old man wasn't following him. Ryan looked back at the three-storey building with the peeling paint and rusty air conditioners sticking out of the windows. He'd never go back.

As he walked along, Ryan shuddered at the memory of the cop's flashlight playing across his body. No way was he going back to juvie to be thrown into a pod with the likes of Dan. Running was the only option, the farther away the better. The cops would expect him to head south. Instead, he'd take the Yellowhead

Highway, going east toward Alberta.

Ryan made his way across town and stuck out his thumb. He hitched a ride with a mill worker driving to Prince George. Sometime later, the guy dropped him off outside of the city at the Yellowhead Bridge.

Ryan walked onto the bridge, which spanned the Fraser River. He watched the water swirl in eddies as it gouged into the riverbanks, pushing gravel and muck around. *It's like my life, all gravel and muck going nowhere*, he thought. He turned and looked down the road. This time things would be different. With determined steps, he walked up the steep slope of the highway.

Chapter 3

Now What?

The dust along the Yellowhead Highway was thick with particulates from the pulp mill. It was the middle of October, but the sun beat down hard. The heat mixed with the sulphur from the pulp mill made Ryan cough as he headed out of town. He didn't give a damn if he breached his court order. He didn't give a damn about anything.

As Ryan looked back across the river, he saw the pulp mill belching its smoke into the air. The people who lived in the shadow of the mill looked like its smoke — grey and gaunt.

Ryan trudged by a convenience store and glanced at his reflection in the window. He figured he looked older than his seventeen years. His mouth was a grim line and his brow was wrinkled. He took off his baseball cap and wiped his forehead. His brown hair needed a wash. Grey shadows showed under his blue eyes. He replaced the cap.

Across the road, he saw the adult prison. It was a fenced, grey-cement structure. People in orange jumpsuits milled around a small outdoor running track.

No way, he told himself, *no damn adult prison will ever see my hide*. His dad was wrong.

Ryan looked up at the never-ending trees in the distance, which he knew hid the Canadian Rockies. Maybe heading east, beyond the mountains, he would find what he was looking for — a fresh start.

A familiar sound brought him back to the

present. He heard it before he saw it. A semi was grinding its gears as it wound its way up the slope.

Ryan pulled down his baseball cap and stuck out his thumb. He hoped he didn't get some nut to ride with. He studied the blue and white plates of the truck as it inched its way up the incline. As the semi made the crest, he saw the slogan on the Ontario licence plate — *Yours to Discover.*

"So far, all I've discovered is that things suck," he said to himself.

Ryan started to run as the dark red semi slowed and headed toward the gravel on the side of the road. His legs covered the distance in seconds.

In a whirl of dust and the smell of diesel, Ryan boosted himself onto the steps and pulled at the handle of the door. He hesitated for a moment before getting in. He gave the trucker the once-over.

A big guy in a baseball cap turned his

way. He wore a T-shirt, jeans, and trendy runners. Ryan figured the guy looked twenty-something. The trucker's smile was wide.

"Don't wait till Sunday to make up your mind. I've got a deadline to meet. My name's Pete."

Ryan made a decision and hopped in. He placed his duffel bag on the floor.

Pete put the semi in gear and they started down the road. "Where you going?"

"I'm heading to Ontario — to work," replied Ryan. "I figured I'd get a first-aid attendant's job in a mill, then maybe fight fires in the summer. By the way, my name's Ryan." He smiled widely at Pete. The trucker was his ticket out. It was best to be somewhat friendly, but not too friendly. Too friendly could lead to accidentally mentioning things like having been in juvie, which might get him dumped by the side of the road.

"City you're leaving is full of mills," said Pete. "There are lots of first-aid positions — nothing there for you?"

"I don't much like the smell of the mills. People in Prince George call it the smell of money. I think it stinks. Bothers my allergies."

Pete's eyebrows raised as he glanced Ryan's way, then he faced the road again.

Taking off his cap, Ryan twisted to place it behind him in the sleeper cab. On the cab's bed were books on psychology and history, plus a bunch of novels. Ryan stared at a pile of books on criminal law in the corner. He had no love for lawyers or probation officers.

Next to the brown leather jacket on the bed, Ryan spotted a folded off-white cotton jacket and pants, with a black cloth belt looped around them. His eyes widened.

As he turned and faced forward, he saw Pete looking at him again.

"You into martial arts — kick-butt movie stuff?" Ryan asked.

"I practise karate to keep in shape, but kicking butt isn't my thing. I'd rather think and talk myself out of scrapes. Fighting is my last option."

Ryan frowned. Most of the guys he knew wanted to kick butt. Even though he had fought a lot in juvie, Ryan had never liked fighting unless he had to. But he never told anyone he didn't like to fight; that would be like asking for it.

Pete's voice broke into his thoughts. "I don't think there's a book on karate back there, but there's other stuff you might like to read. Help yourself."

"No, thanks. They look kind of boring."

"Not to me. Long hauls and layovers — reading gives me something to do."

Ryan stared out the windshield. The woods usually calmed him, but today the forest of short fir trees looked like soldiers in camouflage closing in on the narrow highway. Silence filled the cab for the next fifteen minutes. From the corner of his eye Ryan saw Pete look at him.

"We got four thousand kilometres to cover," said Pete finally. "Hope you're up for some talk. It makes the road go quicker."

Ryan continued to stare out the window. *The trucker seems okay*, he thought, *but he's a stranger who may ask awkward questions.*

Ryan's eyes shifted, and he saw Pete shaking his head.

Ryan decided he'd better come up with something. "Sorry, I'm dog-tired. I've been walking a lot. Just need to catch my breath for a while."

"Man, I know how that is," said Pete. "Sometimes at the end of a long haul, I just want to rest and not talk to anyone."

Ryan nodded.

"Mind if I turn on the radio?"

"Won't bother me," said Ryan.

Pete reached over and switched the radio to the local country station. Songs of lost love, lost jobs, found loves, and misery whined and wailed in the semi's cab.

Ryan looked out the passenger-side window at the scenery and road signs. The rolling hills followed by the mountains matched his mood — up and down like some gigantic roller coaster. He wondered if running was the right decision. Soon it would be too late to change his mind.

Chapter 4

Truck Stop

Two hours of mountains and music made Ryan's stomach growl. He hadn't eaten since last night.

"There's a Husky station up ahead with a truck stop," said Pete. "Hungry? Want to give it a try?"

"Sure." Ryan forced a grin.

The truck stopped at a diner in the middle of nowhere. They got out of the truck and walked toward it. It was a typical truckers' stop — a diner that served thick coffee with a bit of highway wisdom on the side. They sat at a booth and Ryan grabbed a menu. He saw Pete look at the back of his right hand. Ryan had the letters *F-U-C-K-U* tattooed on the backs of his fingers and thumb. Something about the way Pete stared at the tattoo made Ryan's guts churn.

The waitress appeared. Her face was wrinkled and she had a stud in the side of her nose. Around her leathery neck she wore a pendant that said *Grandma Rules*. Ryan wondered if she was an awesome grandma or just a wannabe kid.

"Hi, there. What will it be?" she asked.

"Coffee, bacon, hash browns, and eggs over easy," said Pete. "He'll have the same as me." He nodded toward Ryan. "I'll pay."

"Thanks," said Ryan. The offer surprised him. He wondered what repayment this guy wanted. *No one does something for nothing*, he thought.

The waitress brought them each a mug of

coffee then went to the kitchen, barking their order.

Pete took a slow sip of coffee. "Interesting tattoo you got there," he said over the rim of a dark blue coffee mug. "It looks self-made — lots of wiggly lines. I saw ones like that when I volunteered as a karate instructor at a teen centre. Usually on kids that came out of juvic." He looked at Ryan, waiting for a response.

Ryan took a deep breath. Bluffing this guy was not an option. *Here it goes — all or nothing*, he figured. "I did it my first time in juvie when I was thirteen. I was in for boosting cars. Escaped juvie once when I was fourteen and did more time. Been in and out since then. Did some break and enters — no violent stuff. I guess if you've got a problem with that, then you'll leave me here."

Pete sipped his coffee, then held the mug still. "Ever steal a semi?" He raised an eyebrow and tilted his head.

"No, it's not fast enough."

"Well, that's a relief." Pete's mouth curled into a small grin.

Pete set the coffee mug on the table and rubbed his chin. "Here's the deal. I'll take you east, but after this we share the cost of meals. The room I'll spring for. It's a two-for-one anyway. Some guys think they can bum off the trucker for everything. I won't let you do that. I'm telling you upfront. We'll see how it goes. If it doesn't work out, I promise I won't drop you off in some hellhole. Agreed?"

"Agreed," said Ryan, letting out his breath. "I've got money from fighting forest fires — it was part of a juvie program. I can pay my way."

Ryan figured the deal was fair. But why was this guy agreeing to take him east, knowing he'd been in juvie? He wondered if this guy was some kind of creep.

The waitress placed their breakfasts on the table. "Just pay at the till," she said. More wrinkles creased her face as she smiled. "Enjoy."

Ryan finished everything on his plate. Pete paid the bill and left a tip.

As they walked out of the diner, Ryan looked down at the ragged tattoo on his hand. It was like a neon sign. He stuck his hands in his jeans pockets. He was still mulling things over as Pete unlocked the door of the semi.

Ryan settled into the passenger seat and buckled up. Pete turned on the radio. Country music filled the cab again as they headed toward the Alberta border. Ryan crammed himself against the door, ready in case Pete really was a creep and there was trouble.

The rig moved along. Ryan looked at the lights on the dash that gave a steady glow. He noticed a photo taped next to the glove compartment. It showed a teen and a kid standing on a beach. They looked so similar Ryan figured it was Pete and his brother.

The gears ground as the semi ascended the Rocky Mountains toward Jasper National Park. They passed the sign saying, *Welcome to*

Alberta, and Ryan's shoulders stiffened.

There's no turning back now, he thought. He'd breached his CSO by leaving British Columbia. It would be back to juvie for sure if he were caught. He had to keep going.

His mind spun until he worked out a plan. It was a simple. Run as far and as fast as he could before they knew he was missing. The stopwatch had started ticking.

Tired from worry, Ryan finally leaned his head against the window and fell asleep.

Chapter 5

Highs and Lows

It wasn't until the wipers swished and the truck's heater kicked in that Ryan woke up. Snowflakes were shooting like white arrows toward the glass.

"What's with this? A while ago we were sweating," Ryan said.

"It is weird weather — a bit early for snow in the Rockies. Looks like a Christmas card out there," said Pete.

Ryan looked out at the swirling snow that

circled the forest of fir trees. The forest lay at the foot of towering mountains, whose snow-capped peaks seemed to pierce the sky.

"It looks way better than a Christmas card. Cards suck," Ryan said. "All those stupid things written inside."

"Don't like mush?" said Pete.

"I don't like people writing things they don't mean. It's disappointing. If they cared, maybe they should say it in person."

Pete didn't reply.

The snow began to fall harder. "If this gets worse we'll have to stop," Pete finally said. "It can get pretty wild out there."

"Yeah, I used to live on a ranch in a valley. Sometimes in the winter, we'd get snowed in." Ryan said.

"You lived on a ranch?"

"When I was eleven, I lived with a foster family. The Greens. I came to their ranch just before Halloween. I'd hidden a bunch of firecrackers in my bag. On Halloween night,

I let them off. It scared the horses and almost caused a cattle stampede. I figured the Greens would yell and beat me. Instead, they listened and talked to me and tried to help."

"A stampede, eh?" said Pete, shaking his head. "You were lucky they were kind people."

"I don't know why they didn't send me back to social services. They let me stay. They taught me to ride, herd cattle, hike, and love the mountains. Sometimes we'd just sit around the fireplace in the winter, listening to the howling wind and looking out the window at the swirling snow. It was the first time someone gave a damn about me. Then a forest fire ripped through the ranch and everything fell apart. The Greens left for Ontario. They wanted me to go with them, but social services said I couldn't leave the province. Instead, I wound up in some hellhole where all the people wanted was the money social services gave them. Later, they put me back with my dad."

"Doesn't seem fair that you couldn't go with the Greens," said Pete.

"I had no say about where I lived, who looked after me, my clothes, school — nothing."

"That bad, eh?"

"One place was okay. The people were nice, but I wasn't there for long. It was a short-term emergency home, so they moved me on when they needed the space for another kid. The last one was a real hellhole. The guy was always yelling, using his fists, no patience with the little kids living there. I tried to step in, but he started on me. I kept out of the house most of the time. Sometimes I was gone for days. Not long after that, I ended up in juvie." Ryan's voice had a flat edge to it. He looked out the window.

"Last time I was in juvie, I wrote a letter to the Greens," Ryan said a moment later. "I used their old address, hoping it would get forwarded. I thought they might see me. That they might have a . . ." His voice trailed off.

"A place for you to stay?"

Ryan nodded. "But I never heard back. Another dead end."

"Do you know where they moved to in Ontario? You could search for them when you get there."

"Whatever," said Ryan. "It was just a crazy thought." But deep down he knew he'd keep looking.

Pete didn't ask any further questions.

Ryan wondered why he had told this guy about being in foster care. He didn't like thinking about those years, especially the good times with the Greens. Another chance flushed down the toilet — just his luck. He stared out the window.

Pete switched the radio station and listened to the weather report.

"Nasty weather out there. Not getting any better," he said. "We can pull off at this little town ahead and get an early start tomorrow. The roads will be cleared by then, and we'll make better time."

He slowed the semi as they entered the town. A kilometre down the road, the neon sign of an old motel blinked *Vacancy* through the falling snow.

"We'll stop here. Looks okay, for what it is. Besides I need a shower. It's one thing they don't have in these rigs," said Pete.

They pulled into the parking lot of the old motel. The air brakes groaned and sighed, then were silent. Ryan and Pete jumped out of the cab. Pete walked around the semi inspecting the lines. Ryan checked out the motel. *Probably looks better in a blizzard than in the light of day*, he thought.

They walked toward the office. The old guy behind the desk looked as rundown as the motel. A cigarette hung from his lips, and his grey hair stuck to his head like it hadn't been washed in weeks. As they drew near, Ryan smelled body odour mixed with the cigarette smoke.

Pete paid the guy for the night. He told him they'd be leaving early in the morning, so they'd leave the keys in the room. The guy flicked his cigarette in the ashtray and reminded them they were in a non-smoking room. He told them if they wanted a pop he had some in a fridge. Pete said thanks, and they left.

Pete had to jiggle the key in the lock before the door to their room unlocked.

"Well, any port in a storm," said Pete, flicking on the lights. "As long as it doesn't have the two Rs we're okay."

"Two Rs?" asked Ryan.

"Yeah, roaches and rats," said Pete. He turned on the mini TV and flopped on one of the beds. "Damn, it's tiring watching all that white stuff coming at you. Think I'll relax, have a shower, and turn in early. We need to be on our way by six o'clock."

"Got it," said Ryan. "I'll be ready. But right now I need a pop, maybe some munchies. I saw a corner store when we drove in. You want anything?"

"Yeah, a Coke sounds good. Thanks." Pete leaned back on the pillow and closed his eyes.

Ryan headed out the door.

Chapter 6

Sketchy Place

The piled-up snow crunched under Ryan's runners. He had a hole in the side of his left shoe, and his sock and foot were wet and cold. He shoved his bare hands into his worn jacket and trudged on. The outdoor neon light of the corner store blinked off and on. The thing had a smiley face, now capped by a hat of snow.

Standing in front of the store were three guys with toques on, talking to a fourth wearing a baseball cap. The fourth guy was big, taller than Ryan. Ryan was near enough to see the foursome, but he couldn't hear them. He figured the big guy was in charge — he was up in the other guys' faces.

Ryan took a deep breath. He didn't care what was going down. His problem was they were blocking the door. The big guy shoved one of his buddies.

Shit. How much do I want that pop? Ryan asked himself. *If I turn tail now, they'll come after me. It's just like juvie — boss or be bossed.* He kept walking toward the store.

The big guy turned toward him. Ryan nodded, trying to show he didn't want trouble. The three guys backed away, giving Ryan room to pass on one side of the double door. The big guy held his ground. As Ryan opened one side of the door, the guy gave him "the look." Ryan knew all about "the look" from juvie. The meaning was clear.

This guy figures he can take me, Ryan

thought. *He isn't just checking me out.* Staring right back at him, Ryan kept moving.

His muscles were tense as he entered the store. The door closed behind him. The guy behind the counter had earbuds in and wore a red shirt with *Trev* written on it. Ryan looked around the store. He grabbed a small can of Coke for Pete and a root beer in a small glass bottle. The big guy was still outside the door. Ryan found a can of hair spray and a couple of bungee cords. Carrying his purchases, he went to the counter to pay. Trev kept bouncing to the beat in his head as his fingers hit the cash register.

Ryan put the pop can in a jacket pocket and let the bungee cords hang out of his jeans pocket. He grabbed the spray can and flipped the cap off. Then, cupping the spray can in his hand, he stuck it in the other jacket pocket and held it there. With his free hand, he grabbed the pop bottle.

As he walked to the door, Ryan could see the big guy looking in at him. The other three had moved back from the doorway. Ryan concentrated on the big guy and moved toward the door. If he took out the leader, the rest might run.

Ryan was just out the door when the big guy opened his mouth. "Looks like you got lots of cash to throw around. It's my turn. Hand it over." His beckoning hand came close to Ryan's face.

"Ah . . . sure," said Ryan. "I got it right here."

His hand came out of his pocket, clutching the spray can. He aimed for the big guy's face and shot with full force.

The guy screamed. His hands shot up to his eyes. Ryan doubled his fist over the spray can and punched the guy in the stomach. He crumpled to his knees. The pop bottle in Ryan's hand tumbled onto the ground but didn't break. Ryan whipped the bungee cords out and hog-tied the guy. When he looked up, he saw the three guys standing there with their mouths open. He stuck the spray can back into his jacket pocket, grabbed the pop bottle, and started running. The three guys were right behind him.

Ryan scanned right and left, looking for a way out.

"Wait up," one of the guys yelled. "We're not after you. We want to get away from Fist."

Ryan stopped. He grabbed the bottle tighter, looking for something to break it on. He felt the adrenalin pumping through his body. The guys walked toward him.

"Fist is one badass dude — hassled us all night," said the skinny guy with the black toque.

"Not that we couldn't take him," said the short guy, who had a scar on his cheek. The other two nodded in agreement. "Hey, where did you learn to hog-tie like that? I only saw that at rodeos on TV. Never seen anything so funny."

Ryan's muscles relaxed. "Worked on a ranch."

"We've got to celebrate getting away from Fist. We were going to a party before he caught up with us. Want to come? Wait till the guys hear what you did," said the skinny kid.

"What's your name?" asked the guy with the scar.

"Ryan."

"Call me Rev. He's Cruiser," he said pointing to the skinny kid. "And that's Sparkplug." The third guy nodded his head.

"You guys like cars?" asked Ryan.

"Yeah," said Rev, grinning. "We like them so much, we try out a different one every weekend. Fist always thinks he can pick the fastest ones. Tells us what to do."

Somewhere in Ryan's head a tiny voice said *Leave*. He remembered another party, the one where he got drunk and stole a car. Fun while it lasted, but then he'd landed in juvie with the biggest headache in the world and part of his life gone.

This party didn't have to end that way. He could have a couple of drinks then go back to the motel — no one the wiser. Ryan's mouth felt dry. The root beer looked good, but he might need it later. A voice inside his head warned him that nobody was ever your instant friend unless he wanted something. Ryan hesitated.

"Come on, there'll be girls there," said Cruiser.

That did it — girls. Ryan followed the guys to the party house. Still cautious, he walked on the outside of the group, carrying his bottle at the ready.

The party house was close to the motel. Ryan could hear the noise and music as they neared the place. He followed the threesome up the stairs and inside. The smell of weed mixed with the odour of beer — good times. He looked around the room. The guys weren't lying. Ryan saw lots of girls, but his eyes stopped on the one in the corner. She had long, jet-black hair and eyes like blue marbles. High black boots covered her long legs. She wore the tiniest tee and the shortest skirt Ryan had ever seen. She looked good, so damn good.

Ryan's mouth was dry, and his hands felt slick as he clutched the bottle. The girl smiled his way. She was standing with two blond girls who were beckoning the guys over. The three guys moved toward the girls and Ryan followed.

"Hey, girls," said Rev. "I'd like you to meet Ryan. He hog-tied Fist at the corner store. We saw it all. Would have helped, but Ryan didn't need us."

The black-haired girl smiled. Ryan moved closer to her.

"Would you like some of my beer?" She waved her bottle at him, and then she nodded to the corner of the room where her girlfriends, and the guys were headed. Ryan noticed she wore a silver necklace with the name *Crystal* engraved on it.

Ryan took a mouthful of her beer. He followed her, put his pop down on a table, and grabbed a bottle of beer for himself. Then he sat next to Crystal, thinking it was his lucky day. Nothing could possibly go wrong.

Chapter 7

Good Times

Everyone at the party wanted to listen to Ryan's tale of hog-tying Fist. Crystal kept smiling at Ryan and asked to hear more stories. She offered him another beer. He'd have drunk a whole keg of beer to please her.

They drank for a while, his arm around Crystal. When she stood up, she held out her hand and invited him to dance. Swaying, Ryan got to his feet. Crystal put her arms around his neck, and they slowly moved to the music.

He pressed into her. She smelled of beer and soap. She held him close, and danced slow even through the rap music. He didn't mind one bit.

Next she led him back to the corner where they joined the group sitting on the floor. Rev, Cruiser, and Sparkplug asked Ryan about boosting cars. Urged on by Crystal and the booze, Ryan began to tell stories of hot-wiring cars, fleeing cops, and car chases. The liquor flowed, the pot smoke hung heavy, and a local pusher handed out pills for cash.

"Want to have some fun tonight?" said Cruiser. "We know of a Hyundai Genesis just waiting to be taken."

Somewhere in Ryan's foggy mind, something said, *Don't do it.*

"Hey," said Crystal, "that sounds like fun. Can I come too? I wonder what the back seat is like."

The first thought vanished from Ryan's mind, and another took its place. The new one involved a back seat and Crystal.

"Sure," Ryan slurred.

"You're in," said Cruiser. "You're one of us now. We answer to Mr. Speed. He runs a chop shop hidden behind his garage down on Eighth Street. He gives us money for the cars we boost. Now that you're in, Speed doesn't let anyone out."

"Yeah. No one gets out. We see to it," said Rev, trying to clean his fingernails with a switchblade.

His friends nodded in agreement. Sparkplug clenched his fists.

Ryan's stomach lurched, and he felt sick and dizzy. "I'll be back," he said. "Where's the toilet?"

Rev pointed. Ryan staggered in the general direction. He lurched past four people sitting cross-legged in a corner, puffing on a bong. They were next to a couple making out on a puke-coloured couch. A guy with money in his fist was looking at pills a girl was selling.

Ryan entered the kitchen and stepped over

some guy passed out on the floor. He opened the bathroom door, staggered to the toilet, and barfed.

Then he heard someone behind him. He didn't give a damn who it was.

The door closed. Ryan looked up and found himself staring at Pete, who was sitting on the side of the bathtub.

"Where the hell did you come from?" Ryan slurred.

"Well," said Pete, "a car crashed into the garbage cans outside our room at about four o'clock. I woke up. You weren't there. I figured I'd look for you."

"How did you find me?" Ryan rubbed his head. It felt like a large piece of cement was wedged into his brain.

"I didn't have to go far — loud music, a driveway full of kids drinking and smoking, plus parked cars with steamed-up windows. They may as well hang out a sign saying Party Central."

Ryan turned back to the toilet and retched again.

"So how's it going with you?" asked Pete.

"How the heck do you think its going?"

"I don't know. What I do know is the cops will arrive soon. I guess you can wait for them or come with me. I'm leaving this town in an hour. I put your duffel in the truck in case you wanted to join me."

"Cops," said Ryan. The word "breach" flashed through his mind.

"Yep." Pete stood up.

"Okay, I'm out of here," said Ryan.

He got up from the toilet. His world spun. Pete grabbed him under the arm and opened the door.

Rev, Cruiser, and Sparkplug stood in the doorway.

"Where you taking him?" asked Cruiser. "He saved our asses. He's our bro, and once he's our bro, we don't let him go."

"So now you have two of us bros," answered Pete. "But he's no good to you half-cut. Needs some air. Just going to take him outside."

"Yeah," said Ryan. He held out a shaky hand. "See? Can't hot-wire."

The guys parted and let Pete and Ryan move toward the front door. Pete helped Ryan navigate the steps. The threesome followed and stood in the doorway. One leaned against the door frame. The other two moved over to the porch rail.

"Just going to walk around," said Pete.

As they reached the bottom of the stairs, Pete whispered to Ryan, "We can't outrun them in your condition."

"Sorry, about that, but they're my bros. They won't do nothing," Ryan mumbled.

"You sure about that?"

"Nope," Ryan said, as he looked over his shoulder. The movement made his head dizzy.

"I'll handle them. I'll give you my key fob. It has automatic buttons for the semi's doors and ignition. Think you can make it to the truck if I deal with them?"

"Yeah. But I can help. They'll listen to me."

Pete and Ryan glanced back. All three guys were drunk and ready for a fight. Rev had his switchblade in his hand, and he wasn't picking his nails with it. "It doesn't look like they'll listen to anyone," said Pete.

"I think you're right," said Ryan.

"If you can get to the semi that will help." Pete placed the key fob in Ryan's hand.

Ryan nodded.

"We'll head for that building next to the alley. The alley leads to a lane at the back of the motel. You'll have a bit of time to get to the semi before they get suspicious. Pretend you're going to throw up, and we're going to find a place to do it."

"That's easy," moaned Ryan. "I won't have to pretend. I feel that way already."

He clutched his stomach and bent over.

"Come on bro, let's dump the load over here," said Pete in a loud voice.

Pete guided Ryan into the shadows. As soon as the darkness covered them, Ryan ran for the semi. He headed past a big Dumpster at the beginning of the alley. He was at the spot where the alley met the back lane when his stomach lurched. Holding on to the wall, he barfed again. He felt like he was in a whirling clothes dryer. Hidden by the alley's shadows, he tried to get his balance as he looked back.

The three guys entered the alley.

"You got your blade ready, Rev?" said Cruiser.

"Always," Rev replied.

Ryan shuddered.

Chapter 8

Escape

Pete waited behind the Dumpster. Ryan thought that his body looked relaxed compared to other guys he'd seen getting ready to fight.

"Hey, man, where'd they go?" Rev's voice echoed loudly in the alley.

"To dump a load or something. They'll be back," said Cruiser.

"Don't think so; it's been a while. I think they took off."

Ryan wanted to turn back and help Pete,

but his head was still spinning. All he could do was listen as the guys' voices grew louder. They were closing in on the Dumpster.

"He knows about the chop shop and Speed. Can't let him get away. Speed will kill us," said Sparkplug.

The guys kept jabbering. Ryan figured Pete had a good fix on their location.

Timing was everything.

Pete stepped out from behind the Dumpster. Ryan moved so he could see farther down the alley.

"Hey guys," Pete said. The threesome stopped and stared at him. "I think it's time to return to the party. Lots of action back there." He nodded in the direction of the house.

"Where's our bro, Ryan?" asked Rev. His switchblade flashed.

Pete shrugged. "Not your business. Party looks like fun. You should head there."

"You're not our boss," yelled Rev. He lunged at Pete, slashing with his knife.

Pete's movements were a blur. In seconds, Rev lay on the ground. His friends stared at Pete.

Pete turned and ran down the alley. Ryan took a deep breath and headed for the semi. As Pete caught up to him, they heard police sirens wailing in the distance.

Despite being drunk, Ryan kept up with Pete. "Do you think they'll follow us?" His voice was breathless.

"Don't know for sure. Keep running. The semi is ahead."

When they reached the semi, Ryan pressed the key fob and jumped in the passenger side of the truck. He rolled down the window and heaved. As his head came back inside the cab, Pete got in and sat in the driver's seat. Ryan handed Pete the key fob.

"Thanks for not doing that in here," Pete said. "But if you miss the ground next time, you'll wash the outside of the semi. Glove compartment has a garbage bag. Use it, okay?"

Ryan nodded and grabbed the bag. His head pounded.

"Those guys didn't follow us or they'd be here by now," said Pete. He turned the engine over and put on the running lights. "We got to let her warm up for at least fifteen minutes." He began to check the gauges. "We're going to need fuel soon. We're pretty low."

"There's a gas station over on Eighth," said Ryan, "But we shouldn't go there. It has a chop shop in the back. That's who those guys work for."

They were about to leave when blue lights flashed through the cab. Ryan glanced at the side mirror and saw a cop car pull up and park beside the trailer. The cop got out of his car and walked toward them, making signs to roll down the window.

As Pete rolled down the window, the cop climbed up on the running board. The smell of beer drifted out of the cab.

"I think you two better step out of the cab," said the cop.

The cop stepped down into the snow. Pete and Ryan exited the semi. Ryan came around to join Pete.

"Smells like a still in there," said the cop. "So don't tell me you aren't drinking. Let me see your driver's licence."

Pete handed over his licence. The cop gave him a breathalyser, which he passed with flying colours.

"No sense giving the kid one. It's obvious," said the cop. "So what's the story?" He frowned at Pete.

"Me and my brother have been driving since dawn yesterday. We stayed overnight at this motel. My brother went out for a pop, and I fell asleep. When I woke up, he wasn't back. I went looking, found him at a party house down by the motel, and hauled his ass back here."

"That so?" the cop said looking at Ryan.

"Yes, sir."

"You didn't happen to go by the convenience

63

store down the street, did you? Got a report that some kid was yelling in front of the store. He told the officer he'd been sprayed, but he's always causing trouble. The clerk said the kid and some other guys were hanging around the store, looking for a fight. I guess they found what they were looking for. Someone hog-tied that kid."

"Motel office had pop. I grabbed one, then wandered over to the party." Ryan pronounced each word slowly, so he wouldn't sound drunk.

"Hmm," said the cop. He eyed Ryan up and down, and then glanced over at Pete. Ryan figured the guy was no fool.

"Well, if you hear anything, let us know. I found three of his buddies complaining about a ninja warrior taking one of them down. Sounds like they may have been at the same party as your brother. Busy night, with people playing super cop. Needs to stop. You agree?"

Pete and Ryan nodded their heads.

"Have a good ride, and keep that brother

of yours out of trouble."

"Have a good day, officer. Thanks. By the way, do you know of a gas station open at this hour?"

"Yeah, there's one on Eighth and another on Sixth."

"Thanks, I think we'll try the one on Sixth. I heard the one on Eighth has an interesting backyard."

The cop looked at Pete and nodded.

Ryan and Pete got into the cab. Pete put the semi in gear and hit the road.

They stopped on Sixth to fill up, then headed down the highway. The sun wouldn't be up for another hour. Ryan stared straight ahead with a scowl on his face. From the corner of his eye, he saw Pete looking at him, but Ryan didn't look back. An uneasy silence hung in the air.

Finally, Ryan burst out, "Why did you tell him something was going on behind the gas station on Eighth? Why did you snitch?"

Ryan turned and saw Pete's lips tighten.

His knuckles turned white as he clenched the steering wheel. A street light shone in the cab, giving a ghostly appearance to both of them. The cab smelled of stale beer. Ryan's stomach felt foul and his neck hurt. He rubbed it with the back of his hand.

Pete stared at him for a moment. "Damn, I'm too tired for this crap. Not enough sleep, cops, badasses with knives, and now this. Give it a rest. We need to get far away from that town."

Ryan scowled at Pete. *Screw you,* he thought. But Pete was his ticket out, so he shut his mouth. He rested his head against the window and fell asleep.

Chapter 9

Squealing

They were just outside of Jasper when Pete pulled the semi off at a rest stop and shut off the engine. Ryan did not stir, although he heard the semi stop. Pete left the cab to stretch his legs. When he returned, he climbed into the sleeper cab and fell asleep.

Ryan looked back at Pete. His eyes were closed, and he was rolled up in a blanket. Ryan grabbed a novel and started reading, trying to calm down. He was still upset that Pete had snitched about the chop shop.

Forty pages and one hour later, he was still steaming mad. He opened the cab door then slammed it. He headed to the outhouse. When he came out, he saw Pete walking toward him. Pete entered the washroom, then came out a moment later to join him. Ryan stood in the snow trying to shake the cobwebs from his head. He felt like hell, but at least his headache was gone.

"You feel human?" Pete asked Ryan.

"Sort of," mumbled Ryan.

"Well, 'sort of' has to do. We have to hit the road."

As they got into the cab, Ryan turned to Pete. "Why the hell did you squeal to that cop?"

Pete stared at Ryan "What?"

"I said, why the hell did you squeal to the cop about the chop shop?"

Pete's eyes widened. "You nuts? One guy wanted to stick a knife in me. The other two wanted to beat the crap out of both of us. You said they worked for a guy with a chop shop. Do you really think they're a bunch of guys you'd like to play pool with?"

"We got away, but you went and snitched. If they find out, they'll be after us. You don't squeal. You let it go." Ryan's voice had an edge to it.

Pete shook his head. "What do you think those badasses will do to the next guy that crosses their path?"

Ryan shrugged. "Not my business."

"So maybe I shouldn't have pulled your ass out of that party. Let the cops deal with you. Not my business, eh?" Pete turned over the engine.

The only sound for the next fifteen minutes was the engine warming up. When the semi was ready, Pete rammed the gearshift with more force than necessary.

He edged out of the rest stop into the traffic. Ryan noticed Pete's face was turning red.

Ryan thumbed toward the photo on the dashboard. "That must be your brother in that picture. Well, I'm not him. You don't have to take care of me. I can take care of myself — always have, always will. I bet your brother doesn't like you poking your nose into his business either."

Ryan looked at Pete, who was focused on the road. But something had changed. Pete's shoulders slouched. His mouth had gone from a tight line to a sad curve.

Pete's voice was just above a whisper when he spoke. "My brother, Logan, is dead. He was killed in a car crash two years ago. He was joyriding."

Ryan stared at the road. His body slumped into the worn leather seat. He wished he could disappear like the snowflakes that were vanishing with each flick of the windshield wipers.

This guy's brother's dead and I mouth off at him, Ryan thought. *Why the hell did he search for me? Why did he give a damn?* Ryan's head ached. *What if he dumps me off on the side of the road in a snowdrift?*

Road construction caused them to slow down as they entered Jasper. Ryan focused on the buildings and the train station, trying to forget the whole incident. For a while, it worked. He gazed at the tourist shops. Lying at the foot of the towering peaks, they looked like coloured marbles.

The semi picked up speed on the straight road out of town. Ryan rubbed his neck. It was sore from peering up at the peaks that were trying to punch holes in the clouds. He rolled the window down a crack. Cool air rushed in, but it couldn't blow away the feeling that he'd screwed up. Silence rode with them in the cab like an unwanted passenger. The mountains slid into tree-covered foothills, then deflated like balloons into treeless bumps.

The semi kept burning up the road. They passed the tiny town of Hinton. Signposts and directions ticked off the kilometres. When Ryan looked at Pete again, he had his eyes on the road. But the sadness in his face made Ryan wonder if his thoughts were in the past.

Ryan stared at the straight grooves in the rubber floor mats, trying hard to distract his guilty thoughts. Try as he might, he couldn't stop thinking about Pete's brother's death.

Ryan was a master of silence, but this silence bothered him and he wasn't sure why. By the time they passed the town of Edson, he couldn't stand it any longer.

"I'm sorry about your brother. My mom left just before Christmas when I was seven and my sister was thirteen. My sister tried to look after me, but it wasn't like having my mom. The next year Mom sent a Christmas card saying she loved us and would come home. She never did. Dad always acts like she's dead, maybe she is. I don't know. My sis left when she was fifteen. I have no idea where she is either. Dad drank and beat the tar out of us, especially around Christmas. No surprise it's not my favourite holiday. I guess some of it was my fault. Maybe if I'd been a better kid, Mom wouldn't have left us. It feels like crap being left behind. If your brother's death feels like that, it sucks."

"Yeah," Pete said, "you're right. It does suck."

Minutes ticked by.

"You know, I could have taken care of things myself," said Ryan at last. "But I guess you being there helped some."

"You're welcome," said Pete.

They were silent again, but the unwanted passenger had left the cab.

"You want to listen to some music?" asked Pete.

"Sure."

Pete switched the radio on and they listened to the sound of twanging guitars.

Chapter 10

On the Road

The country music played on as they travelled along the highway. The rolling hills were smaller. The wider prairie was taking over. The sun was out and the snow had vanished from the ground.

The truck ate up the kilometres. On the outskirts of Edmonton, Pete used his phone to alert the company of his incoming delivery. Soon after, they stopped at a warehouse to unload.

"You interested in semis? Want to learn?" asked Pete, as they exited the rig.

"Yeah, I like machinery," Ryan replied. "You'd teach me — for real?"

"Sure."

As they unhooked the trailer, Pete explained how the airbrakes worked and their connection to the compressor. Together they checked the lines, set breaks, and safety features. They left the trailer behind to be unloaded and refilled, then took the truck to a motel.

"You ask good questions," said Pete. "And pick things up quick. I can't let you drive the semi, but I'll show you how it works as we go along."

"Thanks," said Ryan. "I mean it. Outside of school, the only place I ever learned anything was when the Greens showed me stuff. My dad was a good mechanic, but he couldn't keep a job because he was drunk. He never showed me squat. I'm good at auto mechanics, though. Took a course during a semester at school when I wasn't in juvie."

"Maybe you inherited some of your dad's mechanic skills."

Ryan frowned. "Maybe." The idea that he'd actually got something positive from his dad rattled around in his brain as they headed to the motel.

Ryan looked over at Pete. He wondered why it was easy to talk to him about everything. What would it be like to have an older brother like Pete? He missed his sister, but he didn't need to be looked after now. Being with Pete was different.

Ryan looked out the window. What was he thinking? They would reach Ontario soon, and he and Pete would part ways.

The next day they headed toward Lloydminster, on the border of Alberta and Saskatchewan. The earthy smell of fields mixed with the pungent smell of cattle manure drifted through the open window. Ryan was sure it was a place where people helped each other, just like on the Greens' ranch.

They dropped off freight in Lloydminster and stayed overnight. The next morning there was a delay in loading the freight. By the time they headed toward Saskatoon, it was afternoon.

"We're making good time despite the delay, but you never know. Weather across Canada can change like this," said Pete, snapping his fingers. "As you know, it can snow in Prince George right up until May."

"My dad always complained about the weather in Prince George."

"Is he still there?"

Ryan figured he'd already told Pete about his mother, so why not talk about his dad?

"Yeah. We were in the Maritimes when my sister left home. Dad and I headed to the Prairies, and then B.C. He was good with his fists and his mouth when he drank. And he blamed everything bad that happened on me. Social services investigated when I turned up at school with bruises. After that, I never knew who I'd be living with."

Ryan stared out the window.

"Sorry," Pete said.

Ryan shrugged. "Not your fault."

"Not yours either."

Ryan frowned. For as long as he could remember people had told him how rotten he was — that everything was his fault. Teachers nattered that he could do better. His old man always said he wasn't worth spit. Then there was his mom leaving.

Were they all wrong? What if everything isn't always my fault? Ryan thought. *Maybe all I need to do is get away, make a fresh start. Maybe running is the right decision.*

He watched the scenery change as the semi rolled toward Saskatoon. The stubble-filled fields looked like an old man's whiskers. An hour later, a snowy-white blanket covered the flat prairie. Ryan rummaged for a book from the sleeper cab to pass the time.

"You doing anything with those textbooks besides getting eye strain?" Ryan asked as he grabbed a mystery book.

"Yeah, you might say so." Pete grinned. "I'm studying for my degree by distance education. Schedules change a lot when you're trucking. Distance ed is just the ticket."

"Never thought of distance education," said Ryan. "Might be an idea for me."

"Might be," said Pete, nodding.

Ryan buried himself in the mystery book as the kilometres rolled by. Twenty pages later he looked up as they pulled into a gas station with a convenience store.

"You stay in the cab and keep warm," said Pete. "I have to pay anyway. You want anything from the store?"

"I'm good. Thanks."

Ryan watched people come and go. One guy pulled up in a BMW. He parked it away from the pumps, left it running, and walked into the store.

Pete entered the cab and turned on the ignition.

"See that car over there," Ryan motioned toward the BMW. "Dumb guy left it running. It's his own damn fault if someone steals it."

Ryan saw Pete frown as he nosed the semi onto the road.

"When I was in high school, I worked at a garage after school," said Pete. "I figured I'd save and buy an old truck. Thought I'd use it for a second job delivering wood for people's fireplaces. My dad was laid off. The family needed money. Eventually, I bought an old Ford. One day, while I was doing a delivery, I left the keys in the truck. Someone stole it, totalled it, and ran."

"I'd kick his ass if I'd found him," said Ryan.

"I left the truck for a few minutes to deliver wood. I don't think I deserved to have it stolen. I saved for months to get it. I felt angry and then sad when the truck was taken."

"I never thought of it that way." Ryan rubbed his neck.

They stopped to drop their freight in Saskatoon. Pete arranged a pick up for the morning, and then they got a motel room.

That night, Ryan lay awake thinking about Pete and his truck. He wondered how he would feel if someone stole from him. Until now, cars were just things to him. He never thought about how the owners felt.

Did all the people I stole from feel angry and sad? What was I thinking when I boosted cars?

He felt like hell about it now.

In the morning, Ryan still felt awful as he stepped into the rig. He had hardly slept. Pete put the truck in gear and they headed to Yorkton. About an hour later, the flashing lights of a weigh scale came into view. Trucks were lined up. Stuck in line, Ryan asked about the weigh scale's operation. Pete explained the semi would be checked by two inspectors for vehicle safety and weight. As Pete talked, Ryan wondered what it would be like to be a trucker.

They stopped for burgers and fries in the late afternoon. Then it was back on the road. When an RCMP car zoomed by, sirens blaring, Ryan's heart pounded.

By now the cops knew he'd breached. Pete didn't know about the CSO, the breach, or the B and E. Ryan wondered if he should tell him. His conscience would feel better if he told Pete everything.

But I'd be putting Pete in a bad position, Ryan thought. *He'd get in trouble if he didn't turn me in.*

Ryan's mouth remained shut. He continued to read the mystery novel. After an hour of reading, he closed the book and stared out the window — anything to keep his mind off worrying.

Chapter 11

Terror

The truck hummed along, the pitch changing as the gears shifted. The wind picked up outside, rolling over the flat prairie. Tired from worry, Ryan rested his head against the window and fell asleep. When he opened his eyes, he could hardly see outside. Snow was coming directly at the windshield. In fact, it was moving sideways. The semi's headlights were on, but they weren't helping. The world was blindingly white.

"Where the hell are we?" asked Ryan.

"Somewhere outside of Yorkton," said Pete. "I wish I could pull over and wait this thing out. Damn blizzard came up suddenly. Can't see a thing. There are ditches on either side of the road. If we hit one, everything will flip, so I'm trying to follow those tail lights up ahead. I just hope they know where they're going."

Ryan stared through the windshield. Ahead were two red tail lights, burning through the white needles of snow like hot eyes.

He looked over at Pete's tense face, lit by the glow of the dashboard. Pete was gripping the wheel tight with his left hand. His right hand was ready to gear down and slow the truck if necessary.

"Anything I can do?" asked Ryan.

"Not a hell of a lot. But thanks. Just keep your eyes peeled for anything."

Ryan narrowed his eyes, but all he saw up ahead were the two red lights appearing and disappearing in the snow. He glanced at the side mirrors, which reflected the headlights from the car behind them. Looking out the side window he saw a large ditch filled with snow alongside the road. He spotted a sign, but it was a blur of white. He looked out the windshield. The red lights ahead had disappeared. Bright headlights appeared, flashing everywhere. A vehicle was spinning out of control.

"No!" yelled Ryan as a large SUV slid sideways, heading directly for them. Ryan's eyes opened wide. His body tensed. Pete swerved the semi left, trying to avoid the SUV. The semi's trailer began to jackknife. Wheels spun. Metal and gears ground and heaved, wailing like banshees. The eerie lights of the dashboard began to turn sideways. Everything was happening so fast.

Then, roaring and grinding, the semi flipped on its side. It lodged in the ditch and the world stopped moving.

Ryan took a breath. Every muscle in

his body was on edge. He was stuck at the upended part of the cab. He was leaning sideways, held in place by the seat belt. Ryan moved his body. Nothing seemed broken. He looked down at Pete, whose head was against the side window. In the glow of the dashboard he saw blood against the window.

"Pete," Ryan yelled. There was no response. "Pete! Are you all right?"

The cab was silent, just the faint smell of iron from Pete's blood. The odour was mixed with the sour smell of diesel fumes.

Ryan grabbed the dashboard with one hand and the seat with the other so he wouldn't slide down into Pete. Ryan carefully undid his seat belt. He knew that diesel oil wasn't as likely to ignite as gasoline, but there was still a possibility. Working at the ranch had taught him that. No matter what, he couldn't leave Pete.

He balanced himself and checked Pete's breathing. It was low and shallow.

He undid Pete's seatbelt, then scrambled up the cab and shoved his head into the sleeping area.

Ryan pulled out a blanket, towels, and an upside-down first-aid kit. Then he returned to Pete. Lifting Pete's head, he placed a towel underneath, letting the pressure of Pete's head against the towel and the glass to stop the bleeding. He checked for broken bones and searched for anything else that looked wrong.

Then he glanced under the dark dashboard.

One of Pete's legs was at a weird angle and the other was cut and bleeding. Ryan wrapped the bleeding leg with another towel. He slid off his wide belt and used it to hold the towel in place and keep pressure on the leg. Checking Pete's breathing again, Ryan realized it had stopped.

He moved Pete into a better position and began CPR. Ryan tried to breathe life into Pete's body — nothing else mattered. He tried compressions. It was hard to do, but Ryan kept going. He kept a steady compression by following the rhythm of the song "Staying Alive" in his head.

The passenger side door yawed open. A flashlight lit up the cab.

"Get help," Ryan yelled.

"It's okay. I'm a cop. An ambulance is on its way. How is the driver?"

"His breathing stopped. His head is bleeding and his leg too. One leg is at a weird angle. Can't feel anything else wrong."

The sound of a siren pierced the night. Within minutes, the red light from the ambulance filled the semi's cab.

"Keep up the compressions," said the cop.

Ryan kept going. His arms burned and ached. But all that mattered was Pete. The cop left and a paramedic entered the cab. Large hands covered Ryan's. He moved his hands away from Pete's chest as the paramedic took over the compressions.

"Come on, son," said the cop from the

cab's open door. "They'll help him. It will be all right."

Ryan made his way to the cab's open door and joined the broad-shouldered cop.

The man led Ryan to the cab of the ambulance and placed a blanket around him. Then he sat beside Ryan and closed the door.

Ryan's body couldn't stop shaking. He threw up in a barf bag and the shaking stopped.

"It will be okay," said the cop. His voice was calm and kind. "The paramedics are good. They'll take good care of you both. You'll need to go to the hospital with them and get checked over. I'm Constable Davies. What's your name, son?"

"Ryan Jenkins," he said, then gasped. He'd given his real name. What was he thinking? The police computer would tell Constable Davies everything.

A husky paramedic with wire-rimmed glasses rapped on the window. Constable

Davies opened the door and got out. The paramedic got in beside Ryan, a medical kit in his hand.

"That was fine work you did with the trucker," said the paramedic. "Not many people can keep calm." He began to examine Ryan. "Looks like you're okay, but you need a good check at the hospital."

When he left, Constable Davies got back in. He pulled a notepad and pen from his jacket pocket. A small toy car popped out of his pocket and fell on the floor of the ambulance. The cop picked it up. "My son's." He smiled. Ryan tried to smile back.

"You feel like talking?" asked Constable Davies.

"Are the people in the SUV all right?" asked Ryan.

"Thanks to the trucker no one was hurt. Looks like he saved their lives by swerving and missing their SUV. And from what I saw and what the paramedic said, you saved his.

Where'd you learn first aid, Ryan?"

"On a course." Ryan's mind began to race. Here he was sitting with a cop in an ambulance. He felt like crap and his mind was cloudy.

Constable Davies began to ask details about the accident. *Ask away*, Ryan thought. *There's nothing to hide about the accident.* But when the questions ended, then what?

The cop's phone rang. He answered it, then grunted, "I'm on my way." Constable Davies turned to Ryan. "I'll be back in a minute; there might be a problem with the semi."

He exited the ambulance. Ryan watched him in the side mirror. Constable Davies walked down the highway. Eventually, Ryan couldn't see him for the swirling snow.

Chapter 12

Catch and Return

Ryan's neck felt stiff. Every muscle in his body was tense. He wanted to run. If Constable Davies typed in the name Ryan Jenkins on his computer, "wanted" would flash across his screen, then what? The answer was simple. Ryan would go back to juvie. He had to get out of here.

Ryan put his hand on the door handle.

Constable Davies's face appeared at the window. Ryan's eyes widened and his jaw dropped.

The cop opened the door. "Didn't mean to startle you," he said. "The semi is okay."

Ryan made room for Constable Davies to get in. His heart was pounding.

"So, Ryan," said the cop. "Let's continue. Can you tell me something about yourself?"

Ryan decided to tell part of the truth.

When he was finished, Constable Davies rubbed his chin. "Basically, you hitchhiked, you're seventeen, and you're on your own, correct?"

Ryan nodded.

Constable Davies glanced at the rear-view mirror. "I have to check with the paramedics. I'll be back." He stepped out of the ambulance again.

The feeling in Ryan's gut told him that Constable Davies would do more than check with the paramedics. He'd look Ryan up in the police car computer.

Run, Ryan thought.

He looked out the side mirror and saw

the paramedics moving Pete toward the ambulance.

What am I thinking? I can't run, Ryan thought. *I can't leave Pete.*

When the cop returned, he said, "Your friend is critical but stable. You can ride in the back of the ambulance with him."

They walked to the rear of the ambulance, and Ryan climbed in.

Ryan looked down at Pete. An oxygen mask covered most of his face. His head was bandaged, and his eyes were closed. The paramedic's face looked grim. Ryan felt ill.

The ambulance raced down the highway, its siren howling in the darkness.

They pulled in to the emergency entrance of the Yorkton hospital. Pete was rushed to the operating room. A nurse with a kind face took Ryan to the emergency room. He was shown a bed and asked to change into a hospital gown.

The curtains were pulled, but Ryan could hear the patients around him: someone was throwing up; someone else was moaning; and a third person was demanding that she be seen immediately. The smell of disinfectant was everywhere.

The doctor arrived. There were dark circles under her eyes, and she was trying to stifle a yawn. "Long day, busy evening," she said. "Looks like you're not in too bad of shape, but let's see."

After a check, Ryan was told he had to stay overnight and have some tests just to be sure he was okay. When the doctor pulled back the curtains, Constable Davies was waiting. He smiled at Ryan, but there was something in the way he was standing that told Ryan the game was up.

The doctor left, and the cop pulled up a chair in front of Ryan.

"I'm sure you've guessed by now that I know about your CSO. Nothing illegal shows on your record after you breached — that's good."

Ryan stared at the floor. The words "nothing illegal" ran around in his brain. That meant all that worry that some cop in Mill Town had seen his face after the B and E, was for nothing. He hadn't needed to run. Ryan wanted to throw something, pound something, but Constable Davies was sitting in front of him.

Ryan looked out the window as Constable Davies read his convictions. "You have quite a rap sheet," said the cop. "But I don't think you're as badass as the rap sheet says."

Ryan turned and stared at him.

"You just met that trucker a few days ago," said Constable Davies. "You could have taken off after the accident, and you probably wouldn't have been caught. But you stayed, even though it wasn't your problem. You saved a man's life."

Ryan said nothing.

"So here's the deal. You'll go back to juvie and serve the rest of your CSO. But I'll write a report stating what happened at the accident and ask that they go easy on you. The report may help you get out of juvie earlier; or maybe you won't. The judge has to follow the rules. Do your time and keep your nose out of trouble. If not, at eighteen you'll end up in the adult prison. You're a good guy and I really wouldn't want to see you there."

Ryan made a noise in his throat and a half-smile crossed his lips.

"What are you smiling about? I told you, you're going back to juvie."

"It's strange to hear a cop say he cares about what happens to me. Maybe you just don't know me."

"I've seen enough," said Constable Davies. "I know when I'm right. But you have to care about yourself or it won't happen." The cop held out his hand. "Good luck."

Ryan took it. "Thanks."

∗∗∗

Ryan had a restless night. He couldn't get his mind off Pete. When the sun streamed through the window in the morning, the tall burly body of Constable Davies was standing next to his bed. Ryan rubbed his eyes.

"Good morning," said the cop. "Doc says you're good to go. You can see your friend, and then you're off with me."

Ryan dressed and grabbed his duffel bag, which the cop brought from the truck. He walked toward Pete's room with Constable Davies.

Pete had an oxygen tube up his nose. His head was bandaged, and his leg was in a cast. He lay motionless, as if he were sleeping, but it was a scary sleep. Ryan worried, *Would Pete ever wake up?*

Tears formed in Ryan's eyes. He feigned a yawn and rubbed his eyes, like he was still waking up. Constable Davies glanced at him, then looked away.

Ryan never had been much for praying, but he said a silent prayer for Pete. Down deep, he knew even if Pete recovered he'd probably never see him again.

"Anything you want me to tell him when

he wakes up?" asked Constable Davies.

"Just tell him thanks," said Ryan. "Just thanks." He turned toward the door. "Okay if we go?"

"Sure."

They walked out of the hospital to the police car parked outside. When they reached the jail, Constable Davies said, "I hope things work out for you."

"Thanks for everything," said Ryan. "Especially for your recommendation."

"You saved a man's life. You're a hero. I just witnessed it."

Ryan didn't feel like a hero when the cop placed him in the care of the deputy sheriff.

He spent the rest of the day and that night in the local jail. The next morning, he saw the judge, then left with the deputy sheriff on a jet heading west toward Mill Town's juvie.

Ryan had never been on a jet. He flinched when the plane began to vibrate as it sped down the runway. It flew over Saskatchewan's snowy patchwork of fields, then Alberta's oil rigs, which were surrounded by dots of cattle. Each scene was a memory of his journey with Pete, like a film in reverse. Ryan wondered if his luck would change. Maybe he had to make his own luck.

Ryan smiled when the ice-cream capped mountains came into view. Memories flooded in — the Greens' ranch, driving through the Rockies with Pete. His emotions spun around like a Ferris wheel. Some were feelings he couldn't name and didn't want to. The towering peaks were followed by foothills and forest.

When the plane landed in Prince George, he was placed in a van for the drive to Mill Town. As the van got closer to juvie, Ryan shuddered. Darkness crept in. The moon shone like a lantern over the forest, outlining the snow-covered fir trees. It was the last sight Ryan saw as the van reached juvie.

Chapter 13

Inside Looking Out

The brakes of the van ground to a halt in the off-loading bay. A guard approached as Ryan stepped out. He looked up and saw the cold stare of a guard named Mr. Abbot.

Ryan remembered the last time he was in juvie. He'd tangled with a bully, and Mr. Abbot had tried to break up the fight. Ryan had told Mr. Abbot to screw off. It didn't go over well. The fight had caused a lockdown and landed Ryan in solitary.

"You're back again, Mr. Jenkins," said Mr. Abbot. His breath smelled of tobacco. "Face the wall; you know the drill."

Ryan stretched his arms up, placed his hands on the cold concrete, and spread his legs.

"Just couldn't get enough of this place?" said Mr. Abbot, as he patted Ryan down.

Ryan kept his eyes straight ahead and his mouth shut. He tried to focus on the grooves in the pale-yellow concrete bricks.

"I thought you'd be back. You like it here."

Ryan's body tensed. "I hadn't expected to be back here, sir."

"Well, it won't be for long. You'll be in the adult prison before you know it, Mr. Jenkins."

Mr. Abbot spit out the "Mr. Jenkins" like he was spitting out an orange seed. The sound pinged in Ryan's mind.

Ryan took a slow breath and his shoulders relaxed.

"Done. Now turn around." Ryan saw Mr.

Abbot's right eye twitch. His right foot tapped the cement floor.

"Think it won't happen — you landing in adult prison?"

"No, sir."

"Dream on," said Mr. Abbot.

"Mr. Chen will check you in." Mr. Abbot nodded toward a guard Ryan didn't recognize. Probably a newbie. The guy looked like he was in his late twenties. Like the rest of the guards, he wore a dark-blue uniform and light-blue shirt.

"Mr. Jenkins knows the drill. He's a regular here." Mr. Abbot moved to a large desk that looked like a reception desk at a hotel. He picked up a clipboard and started writing.

"I'll get your sweats," said Mr. Chen. "First, let's check in your duffel bag." He had a soft voice for a guard. He looked friendly. *But you never know*, Ryan thought.

Ryan followed Mr. Chen to the desk Mr. Abbot was at. He placed his duffel on its shiny top.

Mr. Chen's black-rimmed glasses slipped down his nose as he rummaged through the bag. Ryan knew what he'd find: a torn winter jacket, too short in the sleeves; a green toque; one pair of jeans with holes; a picture of his sister; a cheap watch; some money he had saved; and a *Go Canucks* sweatshirt he'd bought at the thrift store.

"Do you have a phone? If so, it has to stay in storage."

"Don't have one, sir."

"I had to ask, even though most teens here can't afford one," said Mr. Chen. He continued itemizing the clothes, watch, and picture.

"Is that it?"

"Yes, sir."

"You've got less than most of the kids, which isn't a lot." Mr. Chen shook his head. "You'll get your things back when you leave juvie. They'll send you home by bus. Stay out of trouble when you're out, and you won't see this place again."

"No sense telling him that," said Mr. Abbot putting down his clipboard and turning to Mr. Chen and Ryan. "He likes it here. He thinks it's his home. All he needs to remember are four things. One, no swearing. He had a mouth on him when he was here last time. I cured him of that. Two, address everyone as Sir, Mister, or Ms. Three . . ." Mr. Abbot stopped and glared at Ryan. "No fights. And four, obey the rules. I know you'll break those last two, and when you do, I'll have your hide."

Ryan nodded. There was something about Mr. Abbot's glare that gave him chills. He knew he'd annoyed the man the last time he was here. Now he realized the guy hated his guts and would watch his every move. Ryan wondered if he'd survive juvie. His dad's words, "It will be adult prison for you, mister," bounced around in his mind.

Mr. Chen got sweats and a T-shirt from storage and gave them to Ryan.

Ryan looked down at the grey sweats and

white T-shirt and sighed. He'd never wanted to wear these clothes again. *Well*, he thought, *at least they're warm and comfortable — no holes, so better than my stuff.* He was sure that by the time he got his own clothes back they wouldn't fit anyway. That's what happened the last time he was in juvie.

"Okay, Mr. Jenkins, get changed," said Mr. Abbot. "Then go with Mr. Chen to your pod."

Ryan changed and went with Mr. Chen.

As they walked along the concrete corridors, Mr. Chen chatted.

"We have some new courses. There's a forestry course that's useful."

"Been there, done that," said Ryan. "It was good," he added. "I'll work on my grade twelve instead. I have one course left to complete, then I graduate."

Mr. Chen's eyebrows went up. "Good for you."

They turned right and moved toward the pod where all the tough guys were housed. Ryan's eyes narrowed.

"Keep out of trouble, and they may move you to a better area," said Mr. Chen.

They walked by two guards. When Ryan and other guys had fought, these were the guards who had broken them apart. The men stared at Ryan as he passed.

"I don't think they'll move me," he said.

"You don't know that for sure," said Mr. Chen. "You'll get out of juvie. Things change."

Ryan didn't answer. He was certain something had changed since he'd met Pete. He wasn't sure what, but he felt different. Pete and the Greens had believed in him. He wouldn't let them down. He wouldn't let himself down. This time he was not going to break the rules or fight. Nothing would stop him from getting out of here.

As they reached the entrance to the pod, Ryan smelled the lingering odour of spaghetti from dinner. One thing he liked about juvie was the three meals a day — a lot better than the mac and cheese he'd grown up on.

Dinner was long over, though. The dishes were cleared, and the chairs placed upside down on the tables in the eating area. To his left was a small kitchen with a microwave. Ryan looked around the large room; nothing had changed since the last time he was here. Every pod looked the same. The guys were starting to head to the green doors, behind which were small individual bedrooms.

"I'll see you in the morning. Your bedroom is over there." Mr. Chen pointed toward a green door.

"Thank you," said Ryan. He wondered how long it would take Mr. Abbot to convince Mr. Chen that he wasn't worth spit.

Their voices attracted the attention of the guys going to bed. Ryan froze when he saw Dan and Connor. His mind flashed back to the night of the B and E. First Mr. Abbot, now Dan. Survival in juvie just got harder. The guys nodded at him, and he forced himself to nod back.

Ryan entered his bedroom and shut the door. He changed, flopped on the bed, and closed his eyes. But sleep wouldn't come. He sat up and swung his legs over the side of his mattress. He wondered if Pete was okay. Then he thought of the letter he had sent to the Greens. Had they gotten it?

He lay back on the bed, wondering what the heck his future held.

When he finally fell asleep, the nightmare began. Grinding metal, screaming sirens, and Pete unconscious. Ryan woke up with a start.

After another restless hour, a peaceful sleep mercifully arrived.

Chapter 14

Trouble

The crimson sun rose and shone down on the concrete prison. Looking out the window, Ryan wished he was outside. He got dressed and made his bed. He didn't need instructions on the prison's way of making a bed. He remembered from the last time he was here.

Out in the eating area, Ryan got his tray, picked up his breakfast, and sat down at a table. When he looked up, he saw Dan and Connor headed his way.

"Great," said Ryan under his breath. "Just what I need." But he smiled at the guys as they sat down across from him with their steamy scrambled eggs and bacon.

"So how'd you two land here?" Ryan asked, trying to make his face neutral.

"Cops caught us on a B and E." Dan's thin lips tightened and his dark eyes narrowed. He nodded towards the far corner where a blond guy sat, his broad back facing them.

"B and E?" asked Ryan, playing dumb. "Not boosting cars?"

"We got sick of joyriding," said Dan. "I thought we'd try to get some cash the easy way, so we branched out into B and Es."

Ryan stared at them. He was about to say, "You branched out too far," but thought better of it.

"Connor, get me some juice," said Dan.

Connor got up and moved to the kitchen area.

"I see you still have a servant," said Ryan.

"Yeah, why not? He does what I tell him.

When we're on the outside, he gives me the money he earns, just because I'm his friend. Cool, eh?"

Ryan said nothing. He concentrated on his scrambled eggs.

"Not bad grub here," said Dan, munching on a strip of bacon. "We had spaghetti and tomato sauce last night." He smacked his lips. "Remember that deer I hit with that stolen car? It looked like spaghetti and tomato sauce lying there in the ditch. You and Connor freaked out about the dumb animal." Dan smirked. "I thought it was funny, until the cops showed up."

Ryan almost choked on his scrambled eggs as the image of the mangled deer flashed across his mind.

"And remember that guy I smashed in the face at the mall?" said Dan. "His face looked like spaghetti and tomato sauce by the time I got finished with him. I've been training Connor to fight for me. He's pretty good.

Maybe watching Connor fight will be more fun than beating people up myself. But then," shrugged Dan, "maybe not. I haven't tested Connor out yet, but I will soon."

Ryan nodded at Dan. Connor lumbered over with the juice. He was twice Dan's size, but three years younger. His black hair was cut short. Dan ignored Connor and grabbed the cup. Connor sat down.

Dan leaned toward Ryan. "I heard you got a CSO. I went looking for you to boost cars. I guess you were holed up at your dad's place because of the curfew. Now you're here. What happened?" Dan placed his hands on the table displaying his *YOU ASSHOLE* tattoo. Dan's eyes bore into Ryan.

"I breached and went looking for other opportunities. Made it to Saskatchewan before the cops got me."

Ryan didn't say any more. Instead he changed the topic. "Who is in juvie that I should watch out for?"

Dan nodded again toward the big blond guy sitting at the corner table. "His name's Nathan Carter. He was supposed to do the B and E with us. He's a computer wiz. Figured I'd use him to fix the alarm. But he bailed on us. The alarm went off. The cops caught us. Now we're in juvie. It's his fault we're here." Dan's fists tightened.

"Why did he bail?" asked Ryan.

"Something about babysitting because his mom's working two jobs since his old man left. I think he lied about being busy, though. A few days ago, he wound up in here for another B and E."

Ryan looked at Nathan, sitting alone. He doubted the guy could disarm an alarm.

Another guy who's going to look like spaghetti and tomato sauce, Ryan thought. He was sure if Connor didn't beat him up badly enough, then Dan would finish the job.

"When are you getting out?" Ryan asked, hoping he was out before Dan.

"Connor and I got four months each. What about you?"

"I won't know until my hearing comes up."

Mr. Chen interrupted the conversation by asking everyone to line up for class. He nodded and gave a half-smile to Ryan.

As Ryan stood, he noticed Mr. Abbot was watching him. His eyes were narrow and his brow was wrinkled.

Ryan went to the back of the line while Dan and Connor manoeuvred close to Nathan. When Nathan looked behind him, Dan gave him "the look."

As they moved along the hall, Ryan saw Dan crowding Nathan. Then he whispered in Nathan's ear.

Boss or be bossed, nothing changes, Ryan thought. *Keep out of it, and just play along.*

As Ryan entered the classroom, the teacher Ms. Standish smiled at him and he relaxed. He nodded back and took a seat. He'd never caused her trouble. She was fair and didn't judge.

The students opened their books and worked individually. While waiting for his book, Ryan looked around the room. The juvie classroom looked like a regular one. Except here there were no designer clothes, cell phones, or girls. No buzzer announcing that you could go home. Ryan looked at the calendar on the wall — October 29. He sighed. How long would he be locked up this time?

"Hello, Mr. Jenkins," said Ms. Standish. "I heard you were here. From our records and school reports, I see you have only part of a math correspondence course left to do. You'll be my graduate this term."

Ryan smiled. "I hope so."

The teacher handed him the grade twelve math book. Ryan began to work.

The classroom was quiet. Ryan gave his eyes a break and gazed toward the door with the glass pane. He saw Mr. Abbot looking into the classroom, watching, checking for trouble.

Chapter 15

Chances and Mistakes

When the class ended, Mr. Chen and Mr. Abbot entered the room.

"Everyone has an hour of free time," said Mr. Chen. "You can choose the gym or the library. After that, it's dinner. Those going to the gym, line up with me. Mr. Abbot will take the rest of you to the library."

Ryan walked over to Mr. Chen. "Have they added an auto mechanics course?" he asked. "I took one during a semester at school."

"I'm afraid not, Mr. Jenkins," said Mr. Chen, smiling at Ryan. "It's a great idea, though. I'd like to take something like that myself. I've been helping a friend with his dragster. Be great to know more about mechanics. Hopefully, they'll offer that course someday. For now, Mr. Jenkins it's either gym or library. Tomorrow your group does the same thing. The day after that, you guys go to the woodwork shop after class."

"I'll opt for the gym. Thanks."

"Good choice — keeps you healthy, builds muscles."

"Yeah, I like that."

Muscles also keeps the badasses away, Ryan thought.

* * *

The next day, Mr. Chen walked Ryan to a counselling appointment.

"You know that dragster I was telling

you about?" Mr. Chen said. "We're having problems, and I was wondering if you could help. I could bring photos, drawings, manuals, whatever we have, and describe the problems to you. We could teach each other. Maybe we can both learn something."

"Sure, that would be great." Ryan was surprised Mr. Chen was taking an interest in him, especially with Mr. Abbot around.

They arrived at the medical area and counselling offices. Mr. Chen took him to the counsellor's door, where another guard let Ryan into the office. Ryan was relieved to see his old counsellor, Raj Singh. He didn't want a new counsellor who didn't know him at all.

Raj sat behind an office desk, dressed in a sports shirt and jeans. On a chain around his neck was a small red alarm button known as a spider.

"So, Ryan, it's good to see you," said Raj. "I only wish it were under better circumstances. How are you?" Raj had a gap between his two front teeth.

"I could be better," replied Ryan. "I just want this to be over with. Any idea how long I'll get?"

Raj had always been straight with him. He had taught Ryan not to lose his cool. He'd shown him how to breathe, relax, and think when guys got in his face. Ryan trusted Raj.

"I'm afraid not, sorry. It depends on what happened when you breached. We can't discuss that until after court. I don't want to testify against you. I'd have to if you told me you did something illegal during that time."

The sound of the emergency alarm made Ryan jump. Lockdown. Ryan looked at the office door, which had a window. He saw a guard staring at him.

Ryan turned toward Raj and they both shrugged. Somewhere in the building guys were beating each other, and guards were breaking it up. *Never again*, Ryan thought.

"I guess we're going to be here till the lockdown is over," Raj said. "Good time to pick a topic that will last."

Ryan's thoughts raced. What was he going to talk about? Maybe he could tell Raj about Pete.

"I have this friend, Pete. He's hurt bad and in hospital. I'm worried about him. I'm not sure how badly he's hurt."

Raj leaned forward. "I'm sorry, Ryan. It must be hard. Could you tell me more?"

The worry tumbled out of Ryan's mouth, like a river bursting its banks. "I wish I could be with him, but I'm here in juvie. Thing is, I'm not sure Pete would want me as a friend if he knew more about me. He doesn't even know I'm in juvie. Plus, I'm always screwing up, making mistakes. Nobody wants to be friends with a screw-up."

"Tell me, Ryan, do you know someone you like who made a mistake?"

Ryan thought for a moment. "Yeah, my sister. When we were in elementary school, she stole one of my comic books. I saw her in the schoolyard, trading it for some kid's lunch. She shared the lunch with me. But I was really mad and sad because she didn't ask me if she could trade my comic for food."

"Did you forgive her?"

"Eventually. She's my sister. I found out later she'd been selling her own stuff to get food for us at lunch. There was never anything in the fridge at home. She ran out of her own stuff to sell and started in on mine."

"So she made a mistake. But you cared about her and you forgave her."

"Of course."

"Do you think she learned anything?"

"The next time she asked me if she could trade another one of my comics."

"Have you learned something from your own mistakes?"

"I guess. I realized I hurt people, made them sad and angry when I stole. I didn't think about that before." Ryan looked at the floor.

"Would you do that again?"

Ryan looked up at Raj. He thought about

Pete and his stolen truck. "Never again."

"So your sister made a mistake and learned something and so did you. Maybe mistakes are how we learn."

"Yeah, maybe so."

"You forgave your sister. You let it go. Do you think people should forgive themselves?"

Ryan paused. "I never thought about that before."

"Sometimes, when it comes to letting things go, we're harder on ourselves than on our friends and the people we love. You might consider being a good friend to yourself like you were to your sister."

Ryan nodded.

The lockdown finished and the session came to an end.

In his cell that evening, Ryan wondered how Pete was. He wanted to talk to him, or at least write him, but he didn't know his address.

He thought about their journey together. He remembered the mistakes he'd made. Pete had forgiven him, just like the Greens. After the firecrackers, the Greens had trusted him, and he tried not to let them down. Ryan sighed.

Maybe I should forgive myself and start over, he thought.

Chapter 16

Partners

A few days later, Ryan entered the eating area for breakfast. As he fell into the routine of juvie he started to relax. He wondered if this time juvie wouldn't be too bad.

He spotted Mr. Abbot standing by the wall near the juice dispenser. He was talking with Mr. Chen. Ryan heard Mr. Abbot's gravelly voice as he drew near.

"Jordan Jones, that kid in the other pod you mentioned. Go easy on him. He's got challenges and doesn't always understand. He reminds me of a cousin of mine who has difficulties. We have to explain things to him, kind of watch out for him."

Ryan glanced at Mr. Abbot. *Abbot's concerned about that guy?* Ryan thought. *Maybe he's changed.*

But as Ryan passed by the guards, Mr. Abbot said, "I don't want any trouble from you, Mr. Jenkins, or you'll find yourself in solitary faster than your head can spin."

"No trouble, sir," Ryan answered.

He took a deep breath. *I guess that change doesn't apply to me.*

Ryan got his breakfast and walked to the back table. He noticed Nathan sitting by himself. Dan and Connor sat with a group of guys at the other end of the room. Ryan watched as Dan glanced Nathan's way. Then Dan turned his back on Nathan and whispered to Connor and the group.

The guards were busy chatting and

drinking coffee. They seemed unaware that trouble was brewing. Ryan figured Connor was like a chauffeur, and Dan was his boss riding in the back seat, giving directions, and telling him what to do. But if anything went wrong, it would be Connor's fault.

"All right, people," said Mr. Chen, "line up. We're heading to the classroom."

Ryan made sure he was at the end of the line, away from Dan. When they got to the classroom, he was the last to enter. He glanced behind him as the door closed and saw Mr. Chen looking through the door's window. The guys were just settling into their seats. Ms. Standish was busy helping a student. Nathan took his seat, opened a notebook, and started writing. Ryan looked around for Dan. No way did he want to sit near him.

But Dan was walking with Connor toward Nathan. In Dan's hand was a heavy book. As he passed Nathan's desk, he leaned sideways and slammed the book on the desktop. Nathan jumped. He looked up. His face was pale.

Dan laughed. "Scared you, eh?" His voice was loud.

Everyone turned to watch.

"Sorry, Nathan," Dan sneered. "I'm clumsy. You never know what will happen next. Better be careful."

Ryan heard the door open. It was Mr. Chen. "That's enough Mr. Main. I see what you're doing. Come with me."

Dan glared at Mr. Chen. He walked toward him and out of the classroom.

Juvie doesn't change, Ryan thought. He found a desk, sat down, and started working on math. One problem involved distance and speed. His mind bounced to the semi and Pete. But the images of Pete faded as he continued working and focused on the world of math.

Ryan heard a bang behind him. Startled, he spun around, ready for anything.

He let out his breath. It was only Ms. Standish picking up her cane from the floor.

"Sorry, I came up behind you," she said. "Most people hear me coming from a distance." Ms. Standish had a slight limp, the result of a recent skiing accident. "You're a good worker, Ryan. You'll finish this course in no time. If you don't mind, I'd like you to take fifteen minutes at the end of each class to teach Connor."

Ryan minded, he minded a lot. He didn't want anything to do with Connor, because with Connor came Dan. But the voice inside Ryan's head said, *Don't make waves.*

Ryan nodded. "That's fine."

Ms. Standish showed Ryan how to teach fractions to Connor, then left. Connor looked wary, like a stray cat Ryan had befriended when he lived at the ranch.

After fifteen minutes of teaching, Connor slumped down in the chair. "I just don't get it."

Ryan looked at Connor and sighed. The class ended. Escorted by Mr. Chen, Dan rejoined the group. Everyone walked to the woodwork shop.

Ryan sat next to Connor at the workbench. Connor was carving a bear from a piece of wood. Dan sat across from them. Ryan noticed that Mr. Chen was watching them again through the window in the door.

"How do you do that?" Ryan nodded toward Connor's carving.

"The bear is in the wood," Connor said. "You follow the wood's grain." He traced the outline of a bear on Ryan's piece of wood. "You chisel away the extra wood around it, so you can see the bear."

Dan snickered. "He tells everyone that bear-in-the-wood crap. He's full of it."

Ryan looked at Dan's project. "All I see in front of you are pieces of wood. No bear, no nothing."

Dan's eyes narrowed. "Didn't you hear me? I said Connor's bear-in-the-wood story is crap."

"Until I see you do better, it's not," replied Ryan.

Dan stood up. His fists were on the table.

He glanced at the door and saw Mr. Chen. He sat back down.

Ryan turned to Connor. "Can you help me carve a bear?"

Dan grabbed his own wood pieces, stood up, and stomped off to another table.

"I don't know why Dan says things like that," said Connor.

"He's an ass," said Ryan.

After an hour, Ryan had an outline of a bear's head on a piece of wood, but it didn't look like Connor's bear.

"It takes time," said Connor.

Suddenly, Ryan had an idea of how to help Connor. He asked the woodwork teacher if he could use small pieces of wood to teach Connor fractions in woodwork class. It took a while but the light went on in Connor's eyes as he worked on his fractions.

"It takes time," Ryan said, smiling at Connor.

They spent the rest of the class working on

their bear projects. As they left the woodwork shop and moved toward the library, Dan elbowed his way beside them. Mr. Abbot was in front of the group, writing on a pad attached to a clipboard. Mr. Chen walked behind the guys.

"Look at that dude, Nathan," said Dan. "He thinks he's better than everyone else. Watch this." Dan pretended to fall and pushed Nathan into Mr. Abbot.

Mr. Abbot stumbled. The clipboard clattered to the floor. Mr. Abbot regained his balance and glared at Nathan. "That will cost you, Mr. Carter," said Mr. Abbot. His right eye was twitching.

"Actually, it will cost Mr. Main," said Mr. Chen.

Dan sneered at him, but then the sneer vanished. It was replaced by a wide-eyed look of innocence. "I just fell. It was Nathan's fault. He purposely pushed Mr. Abbot."

"I think not," said Mr. Chen. "That was no

stumble, Mr. Main. It was deliberate."

"Asshole," murmured Dan.

"I heard that. You know the rule — no swearing. Come with me, Mr. Main," said Mr. Chen.

Mr. Chen and Dan left the group and went down the hall. As Ryan and Connor entered the library, Connor whispered to Ryan.

"Mr. Chen has it in for Dan. And Nathan deserved it. So Dan's going to get him. He wants me to help."

"Do you think that's a good idea?" said Ryan.

Connor stared at him, like it had never occurred to him to question Dan's orders. "Dan does," Connor said.

Ryan's brow wrinkled. "I'm sure Dan can handle himself. He doesn't need you."

"He's my bro. I have to help him," said Connor.

"I'm your bro too," Ryan heard himself saying. He wondered why he had said that.

He stopped himself before he could say anything else. As sure as spit hits the ground, Ryan knew there was going to be trouble.

Dan was going to get Connor to beat up Nathan. *Should I step in and help Connor? No way*, Ryan thought. *I want to be far away when it happens.*

Chapter 17

Hidden Answers

Ryan watched as Nathan was bullied by the guys in the pod, thanks to Dan's prodding. He wondered how long the taunting would last.

Ryan hadn't been paying much attention to Nathan. He'd been too busy trying to avoid trouble. But now he wondered about the big, blond guy. *Why doesn't he stand up for himself? What the heck is he waiting for? Boss or be bossed, that's the rule. The longer it goes on, the worse it gets.* Ryan had learned to stand up for himself.

Nathan would have to do the same.

Ryan decided that all he could do was watch as the tension in the pod spread like a disease.

The guards broke up minor incidents. Mr. Chen talked to Dan, Connor, and Nathan, but nothing changed.

Mr. Abbot continued watching Ryan like a buzzard scanning the ground for his next meal.

One morning, Ryan was by himself at breakfast when Mr. Abbot came up to him. The guard pulled out a chair, swivelled it around, and straddled it. His upper lip curled, showing his tobacco-stained teeth.

"You sit there looking as innocent as heck," he said to Ryan. "But I know you. You're causing all the trouble in this pod. For now, you're getting away with it, but not for long." He paused and coughed. "I know you're smart. You use your brain to cause trouble. When you slip up, I'll be there."

He got up, and walked away, leaving Ryan with a tightness in his gut.

A second later, Ryan saw Dan coming his way. He sighed.

Dan plopped down on the seat in front of him. "What did Abbot want?"

"Oh, the usual. Keep out of trouble. He says that to everyone."

"Not to me," said Dan. "He's got it in for you."

"It's nothing." Ryan saw Mr. Chen glancing his way as he talked to Mr. Abbot.

"Whatever," said Dan. "Abbot's got his favourites to pick on — and you're one. He never picks on dumbasses like that new kid, Jordan. Kid's as dumb as a board, doesn't even remember the routine. It's like watching a goldfish circling a castle in a bowl. It keeps saying to itself, 'Oh a castle, oh a castle.' Jordan's even worse than Connor. At least Connor knows the ordinary stuff and gets me juice. I can talk to him. Lot of dumbasses in here, but you and I aren't like that."

Ryan looked at his breakfast and nodded. He looked up to see Mr. Chen coming their way.

"Mr. Jenkins," said Mr. Chen, "would you please come with me?"

Ryan stood, thankful to get away from Dan. He followed Mr. Chen outside of the eating area, and then they stopped to talk.

"You have an appointment with the counsellor in an hour," said Mr. Chen. "Would you like to spend the next hour with me going over some photos and manuals I brought for the dragster? Maybe solve some problems? The library is available."

"Okay." Ryan smiled.

Ryan was surprised when Mr. Chen said it was time for his counselling appointment. The hour had passed quickly.

As they walked down the hall, Mr. Chen thanked Ryan for his help.

"It's good to have someone to talk to about

mechanics," said Ryan. "The guys I hung out with talked about boosting cars, not fixing them. A friend started teaching me about semis. I enjoyed it."

"You're really good at mechanics; maybe you'll be good at engineering."

"Thanks."

Mr. Chen unlocked the door leading to the medical area and counselling offices. Ryan sat on a bench next to the medical room to wait for Raj.

Mr. Chen entered the medical room, but didn't quite shut the door. It was open enough for Ryan to hear him talking to the nurse inside.

"What do you know about Connor Cog? He seems so easily influenced by others in his pod," said Mr. Chen. "If I knew, it might help."

"Don't be too hard on him," said the nurse. "He's just an average kid, does okay in school, but it must be a struggle. He has a learning disability in math, but I guess it's the FASD that affects him."

"Thanks, knowing that will help," said Mr. Chen. He opened the door and came out of the medical room. He patted down the guy who was leaving Raj's office and left with him, saying goodbye to Ryan.

Raj smiled as Ryan entered his office. They sat down on the cheap straight-backed chairs. Ryan couldn't get his mind off what he had heard. He did not want to ask Raj what FASD was. He shouldn't have listened in the first place. He decided to talk about his nightmares.

"Nightmares?" said Raj.

"Yeah, I get them sometimes. It's like I'm back at the accident with Pete."

"You were with him? I thought it was just Pete in an accident. Can you tell me what happened?"

"I was riding with Pete. There was a blizzard, and an SUV slid into our lane. No one's fault. Just weather and bad luck. I was scared as hell." Ryan could feel his neck and shoulders stiffen as he told the details of the crash.

"When I saw Pete unconscious, something changed. Nothing mattered but Pete. I gave him CPR until help came. I thought about running then, but I couldn't leave him. I did my best. Everyone did — the cop, paramedics, doctors." Ryan felt his emotions tumble through him as he told his story.

"I'm glad you're okay," said Raj. "And, as you said, Pete is in good hands. You did your best. You made a good decision to stay. And you're right, the accident was no one's fault. All of these things are very important to remember. Those thoughts will help you with the nightmares."

"But the nightmares keep happening. The scary part is at the end of the nightmare, when Pete is unconscious again. I'm worried about him."

"Do you think Pete will make it?" asked Raj.

Ryan paused, then said. "The doctor seemed good. And the paramedic said I helped save his life. So I guess he has a good chance of being all right."

"Remind yourself of that, Ryan," said Raj.

Together they worked on strategies to use the next time Ryan had the nightmare. When counselling ended, Ryan felt better. He continued to think about the counselling session as he walked with Mr. Chen to class.

After class, there was free time. Ryan asked to go to the library. He had to find out about Connor and FASD. It was safer to search for a library book, he figured. A computer would be faster, but they were only allowed in the classroom. They were strictly monitored by Ms. Standish. Ryan didn't want to explain to her what he was searching for. Plus, juvie banned a lot of internet sites.

Ryan searched in the library's reference section. With patience, he found information about FASD, which stood for fetal alcohol spectrum disorder. He began to read. He finally closed the book and sighed. FASD meant that if a mother drank alcohol while pregnant it could cause brain damage to her unborn child.

As he lay in bed that night, Ryan looked out at the clear, dark sky, studded with stars, and he thought about what he'd read. He resented his mom for leaving him, but at least she hadn't drank.

What would I have been like, Ryan wondered, *if my mom didn't know she shouldn't drink when she was pregnant? Or was too screwed up to know what she was doing? Would I be like Connor, following guys like Dan? Never realizing when people were using me?*

Ryan knew Connor had feelings and could reason like everyone else. But in some situations, Connor couldn't figure things out. It was because he had FASD. Then Ryan thought about Jordan, who couldn't remember a simple routine. He was a lot worse off than Connor. Ryan figured Jordan had a more serious problem.

For once in his life Ryan felt lucky, and he silently thanked his mom.

Chapter 18

Down the Drain

Ryan's patience grew as he continued to help Connor. But every time they were together, Dan glared at them. As Connor worked on fractions in class one afternoon, Dan snickered from the back of the room.

Connor looked back, then turned to Ryan. "Dan thinks I'm dumb," he whispered.

"You can figure things out, Connor," replied Ryan. "Only smart people do that."

"Thanks, Ryan. I'll keep trying."

Ryan was glad that Connor was doing better. But he wondered just how long it would take for Dan to attack Nathan and use Connor as an enforcer. He didn't like the idea that Connor was being used.

After class, accompanied by guards, Connor went to the library and Ryan headed to the gym. He was minding his own business, when Dan started lifting weights beside him.

"You down with getting Nathan?" asked Dan.

"Not my problem," said Ryan.

"Maybe I'll make it your problem. You're either with me or not. If not, you've got a problem."

Ryan faced Dan head on. His eyes narrowed and his muscles tightened. "I don't care what you do, Dan," he hissed. "But leave me out of it, or you're the one who will have a problem."

Dan looked up at Ryan. His stocky shoulders were squared, and his hands were in fists. There was a sneer on his face.

Ryan's eyes stared into Dan's. Finally, Dan blinked. The sneer disappeared.

"Just don't cross me, or get in the way," he said. He strode off to the farthest corner of the gym.

Ryan knew he'd won for now. But the next day was anyone's guess. He continued to watch every move Dan made.

***

When Remembrance Day rolled around, Ryan wondered if the service's message of peace would cool Dan's temper. A short service was held in a room that served as the chapel. Ryan stood at the back. The guys in front of him looked like an army in uniform — everyone in the same tees or sweats. The chaplain, who Ryan thought looked as old as Moses, read from the Bible. Someone recited John McCrae's "In Flanders Fields." The service ended with "Taps" playing on a CD.

As they filed out of the room, Ryan heard Dan say to Nathan, "Your time is coming."

There is never peace in juvie, Ryan thought.

Nathan didn't react. Ryan wondered what kept Nathan going. Maybe it was having someone who gave a damn about him. But was that true? Or had Nathan's family just used him as a babysitter? Did they even visit him?

On the weekend, it was family day. No one came to see Ryan. He walked to the gym with Mr. Chen. They talked about the dragster and made arrangements for a time to meet to work out the problems. On the way, they passed the room where guys visited with their families. He saw Nathan enter the room with a guard and heard a small child yelling, "Nathan, Nathan."

"At least he's got someone," Ryan sighed as he walked beside Mr. Chen.

"Your family doesn't live here?" asked Mr. Chen.

"No one who would come and visit me."

"Sorry, Ryan," said Mr. Chen. "If you need to talk, I can listen."

"Thanks."

"By the way, this came for you the other day." Mr. Chen reached in his pocket, pulled out a letter, and handed it to Ryan. "It got caught in the bottom of the mailbag, so it didn't get handed out. I was asked to give it to you."

Ryan came to a dead stop in the middle of the hall. He stared at the envelope. It was the letter he had sent to the Greens. It had been forwarded to an address in Metcalf, Ontario. But the address had been crossed out, and the message *Return to sender* was written above it. Ryan flipped the envelope over, and saw a second message: *No longer in Metcalf. I think they left for Ireland.*

"Shit, nothing turns out right," he said, bitterly. He crushed the letter in his hand.

"Let's sit down over here," said Mr. Chen, nodding toward an alcove with a couple of chairs.

Ryan's legs felt weak, but he followed Mr. Chen.

"What happened, Ryan?"

Ryan took a breath. "I wrote to a foster family. The only one that ever gave a damn."

Ryan explained about the Greens and the forest fire. Then he added, "They were upset that I couldn't move with them. So was I. I thought if I found them maybe . . ." His voice trailed off.

"Maybe you could live with them?"

Ryan nodded. "But it was a dream. The envelope said they're in Ireland. Ms. Green is Irish, and her family's there. The chance of finding them is zero. I don't know why I thought it would work. Nothing in my life ever does."

"I'm sorry, Ryan. They must have cared about you a great deal to have wanted you with them."

Ryan nodded and was silent. "I think I'll go to the gym."

"Well, if you want to talk, I'm around."

"Thanks."

Ryan entered the gym and joined the rest of the guys. They were the ones no one ever visited. He figured no one gave a damn about them, either. The Greens had cared about him, but seeing them again wasn't going to happen. His fists tightened. He moved to the punching bag and started pounding it.

When he finally looked up, he saw Dan at the end of the gym with a group of guys.

Connor entered the gym.

"Hey, Connor," Ryan said. "Want to spot me with the weights? We can workout together."

Connor grinned at Ryan, then looked at Dan's scowling face. "Sure, Ryan. That would be great."

Ryan saw Dan give him a sour look. But he didn't give a damn how Dan felt. He jerked the heaviest weight and grunted.

When gym period ended, a guard asked

the guys to line up in single file. They then began to exit the room. Ryan, Connor, and Dan were the last to leave the gym.

Ryan had almost reached the door, when Connor suddenly yelled. Ryan spun around to see Dan gripping Connor's shoulder. Connor's face was pale.

Ryan's eyes narrowed.

"Better remember who your bro is, Connor, or else." Dan hissed the words like a snake.

"But I'm your friend," said Connor.

"Remember that." Dan released his grip on Connor's shoulder.

Dan glared at Ryan. "Connor only has one friend — me, not you."

"I'll be friends with whoever I want," said Ryan. "Stay out of my way." He turned and pulled the door hard. It crashed against the inside wall as he exited. Connor scurried after him.

A cry of "Screw you!" echoed from the gym, followed by a rolling cloud of street language.

Mr. Chen entered the gym. Before the door closed, Ryan heard him say, "Stop right now."

As Ryan and Connor headed down the hall, Connor asked. "Why did Dan hurt me? What did I do? He makes me nervous." Connor rubbed his shoulder.

"You didn't do anything. It's Dan's problem," said Ryan.

Connor frowned.

Lying in his bed that night, Ryan replayed the day over in his mind.

Why do these things happen to me? he thought. *The Greens are gone forever. Now I'm mixed up with Dan and Connor. I should have stayed out of it, walked away.*

But somewhere deep inside he knew he couldn't. He wished the days would move faster. He wanted to be out of juvie.

"I don't want to do this anymore!" Ryan yelled, ramming his fist into his pillow.

Chapter 19

Court

For Ryan, the days moved like a slow-dripping tap — just the same routine. There was no hanging out with friends, going to a mall, walking down a street — just schedules and trouble.

Ryan watched as Dan harassed Nathan. He wondered when Dan would make his move.

But, Ryan decided, he had to get on with his own life. There was no sense wasting time and energy figuring out when Dan would erupt.

Ryan was surprised when Mr. Chen pulled

him aside and told him his court date would be the next day, on November 26.

"I guess tomorrow's as good as any other day." Ryan let out his breath.

"You okay?" asked Mr. Chen.

"Yeah, I haven't thought about court since I got here. Too much going on. I guess whatever happens, happens."

"I hear you. I know you must be nervous, but you can do it. Good luck, Mr. Jenkins."

For the rest of the day, Ryan thought about the trial. Had Constable Davies recommended leniency in his report? Who would the judge be? Hopefully, not the one he had last time.

As Ryan got ready for bed, thoughts of the trial the next day still banged around in his brain like a bunch of empty pop cans. He tried to calm himself and breathe. His mind finally turned off and he went to sleep.

In the morning, Ryan was thankful he'd slept. Thanks to Raj's advice, the nightmares seemed to have stopped.

After breakfast, Mr. Abbot escorted Ryan to the loading bay. The deputy sheriff's car was waiting to take him to the courthouse.

"Mr. Jenkins, your time has come to ante up. I'm sure the courts will deal with you fair and square." Mr. Abbot smirked.

Ryan didn't reply. He got into the back seat of the car. The deputy sheriff took him to the courthouse, then put him in the cells to wait his turn.

There were four adults and three teens in the cells. Ryan was put in a cell with another teen. He sat down on the cold orange plastic bench attached to the pale-yellow cement wall. There was a short concrete partition that hid a stainless-steel toilet with no seat. Across from Ryan, there were bars.

The teen next to him kept looking around the room. Ryan figured the guy was looking for a window to escape, but there wasn't one. The teen's legs shook, and his hands kept making fists.

Ryan felt stressed after two hours of sitting next to his nervous cellmate. He was glad when the guard came and took him to the interview room to meet his lawyer. He sat down and looked through the reinforced glass as his lawyer entered the room. The man was dressed in a grey suit. He put his worn briefcase on the small table, opened it, and took out a file.

"We meet again," said the lawyer. With his long nose and slick brown hair, he reminded Ryan of a hawk.

"This time you breached a CSO?" The lawyer's fingers tapped the table.

"Yes," said Ryan.

"Can you tell me anything that might help your case?"

Ryan sighed. "There was a cop in Yorkton. He said he'd write a report asking for leniency, due to what happened on the road."

"I never received any report. What happened?"

Ryan did not answer. His shoulders

slumped. *People never keep their promises*, he thought.

The guard rapped on the Plexiglas door and said, "Time to move to the holding area."

"Looks like your case is going to be heard. Ready?" asked the lawyer.

"I guess," Ryan replied.

The guard took Ryan to a separate cell close to the courtroom. *Another Plexiglas container*, Ryan thought. Ten minutes to go. He felt like throwing up.

As Ryan entered the courtroom, he looked up at the judge. *Damn*, he thought, *it's Judge Allworthy*. The judge who had given him the CSO.

The judge looked down at Ryan. The look in his eyes told Ryan he recognized him. Ryan's brow tingled with sweat.

The Crown presented its case, listing Ryan's previous convictions and ending with his breach of the CSO. *Might as well tell the judge to throw away the key*, Ryan thought.

Ryan's lawyer asked the judge to consider Ryan's time served in juvie, plus the time he'd already served in the community. But nothing positive was mentioned.

The judge turned to Ryan.

"Last time I saw you, I thought you could stay out of trouble. Work on yourself. Is that correct?"

"Yes, Your Honour." Ryan looked up at the judge sitting at the high desk.

"Why did you run?"

"I saw a B and E. I was scared. I didn't want to be sent to juvie for something I didn't do. When I got home, my dad kicked me out of the house."

"That's honest. It's too bad you ran. The report says the officer saw you, but a witness in the house across the street said you had nothing to do with the B and E. She saw you standing across the street as the alarm went off." The judge smiled. "Next time, when you're in a situation like that, remember that everyone gets frightened. Being scared can make it harder to think. Try to calm yourself so you can think things through."

Ryan nodded. He'd forgotten all about the lady in the window he waved to. He'd panicked.

If I get in a tight situation again, he thought, *I need to remember the judge's idea.*

"In one respect," said the judge, "I see you have improved."

Ryan looked up, his eyes wide.

"I received a copy of a report from a police officer in Yorkton. It got waylaid and only arrived on my desk this morning. Apologies to both counsels," the judge said, nodding to the lawyers. "It seems you're a hero, Mr. Jenkins. You saved a man's life when you could have run."

Ryan watched his lawyer's mouth drop open in surprise.

"It does not excuse your breach," said the judge. "But I see hope, Mr. Jenkins, lots of it. Which is good, because your eighteenth birthday is coming up at the end of January. Mess up again, and it's off to the adult prison. You've almost spent enough time in juvie to finish your CSO. So I am going to give you an early birthday present. New Year's Day, you'll be released. You'll be on probation until just before your birthday, during which time your probation officer will help you get back into the community."

"Thank you, Judge Allworthy." Ryan's smile was wide.

"You're welcome. And I hope I will never see you again under these circumstances."

"You won't, Judge Allworthy."

On the ride back to juvie, Ryan felt elated. *Just stay out of trouble*, he told himself.

Mr. Chen was there to meet the car as it pulled into juvie. "You've got a big smile on your face, Mr. Jenkins. Care to share what happened?"

"I'll be out on New Year's Day," said Ryan,

disbelief in his voice. "There was an accident in Yorkton. The judge called me a hero for saving someone's life. I can't believe it."

"I can." Mr. Chen smiled. "I'm sure things will go as smooth as ice from now on."

Ryan wasn't sure about that. You could fall on your ass on ice or fall through. This was juvie and the ice was thin.

Ryan tried to block the thought. He was leaving juvie. He needed to figure out what to do next.

Chapter 20

Plans and Problems

Ryan felt relieved court was over. Now he could make plans for the future. He wanted things to be different this time.

In juvie, everyone told him what to do and when to do it. Every time he got out, he couldn't make a decision for himself. This time he had his own ideas.

At his next counselling appointment, Ryan entered Raj's office and burst out, "I've figured out a plan for after juvie."

"Okay." Raj nodded. "I heard you're getting out."

"I don't want to be ducking my dad's fists anymore. Juvie will give me a bus ticket home, but I'm worried I'll end up on the street. I think I've got enough money for a month's rent. I'll find a job — take anything. I'll save for school — become a mechanic or an engineer. I was hoping you'd help me."

"I'll help all I can," said Raj. "However, things have changed. Your probation officer phoned this morning. Your dad's left town. We don't know where he is."

Ryan stared at Raj. "No more fights and fists?" He paused and looked at the floor. "It's weird. I'm glad he's gone. But he's my dad, and it bothers me that he left. I know it's not my fault. It's just what people in my family do." He looked up. "So what happens now?"

"Your probation officer wants your input. Her ideas are similar to yours — get a job, go to school, learn some life skills, and find a place to stay. There are programs that help with things like the cost of housing."

"Good." Ryan smiled.

"You can apply and have interviews with social services or a housing society for teens and young adults. They will let you know if you're accepted or not."

"I'll apply for both. If I don't get either, I'll need a job. But who will hire a guy from juvie?" Ryan rubbed his neck.

"No one will ever know. Your records are sealed."

"Really?" Ryan wondered what it would be like to not have a record. "I'll still need some help getting a job and a room. I've never done either."

"Ms. Standish and I are here for you. She knows you're getting out."

"Great." Ryan was quiet.

"What is it, Ryan?"

"It's all coming so fast. It's a bit scary."

"Everyone gets scared. It's okay. Until your next session, think of times that you've been worried or scared and you've gone ahead anyway. We'll talk further next time."

As Ryan waited on the bench in the counselling area for Mr. Chen, he thought about his talk with Raj. He had been scared and worried during the accident, but he'd helped Pete. He'd do it again, even though it meant landing in juvie. He'd helped Connor, knowing it angered Dan. He never would have done that in the past. Could he survive the future? A voice in his head said *yes*.

Mr. Chen walked Ryan to his class. But as Ryan entered the classroom, his good thoughts vanished and wariness took their place. Dan was staring at him.

Ms. Standish asked Ryan if he would like to use the computer. "I'm happy to help with whatever plans you have," she said.

She showed him an Internet site for a B.C. government program that would pay his tuition because he'd been a foster kid. *Apply at nineteen*, he read. There were also other grants and loans.

Survive a year, then I can get an education, he thought. *I can do this.*

After class, as he headed down the hall to dinner, Ryan looked out a window. The sky was dark and heavy with clouds. A storm was coming. That evening a cold blast of Arctic air sent the temperature in a nose dive and everything froze. Ryan overheard the guards talking.

"Roads are slick as a hockey rink," Mr. Abbot said to Mr. Chen.

"Glad I've got the night shift," said Mr. Chen. "I think it's going to be worse tomorrow."

As Ryan lay in his bed that night, he heard the wind howling. It banged around the building like a thief looking for a place to get in. The blizzard reminded him of the night of the accident. He fell asleep. The nightmare began. Images of the accident flashed in his head. The truck tipped on its side. The smell of diesel and blood in the cab. Pete slumped against the window.

Ryan sat straight up in bed. Sweat ran down his armpits. He remembered the tips Raj had given him on dealing with the nightmare. "Focus on something in the room," Raj had said. "It will remind you of where you are now."

Ryan looked at the juvie sweatshirt at the end of his bed. He knew he was not in the middle of the accident. He grabbed the piece of paper that Raj had given him when they'd figured out a better ending to the nightmare. Ryan read what they had written. Then he slumped back onto the sheets, took some relaxing breaths, and fell asleep. Now his nightmare had a good ending, with everyone safe and Pete fine. But when he awoke, the same howling blizzard was still battering the building.

Ryan dressed, made his bed, and went to the eating area. He noticed that Mr. Chen was the only guard in the pod. Ryan looked at the clock. Mr. Abbot should have been there by now.

Ryan got his breakfast and sat at the back of the room. Nathan sat at the table in front of Ryan's, with his back toward him. Dan stood in the centre of the eating area, looking around. He seemed to be noting the lack of guards. A smirk crossed his face. It disappeared when he looked over at Nathan. Ryan's body tensed as Dan looked toward the bedrooms.

Ryan watched as Connor came out of his bedroom. Connor closed his eyes and yawned. When his eyes opened, Dan gestured toward the juice dispenser. Connor's body jerked as he hurried to line up for juice. Dan got his toast, then he and Connor walked in Ryan's direction.

Oh hell, thought Ryan.

In the middle of the eating area, Dan stopped and mouthed something at Connor. Ryan read his lips: "Let's do it." Connor shook his head. He looked at Ryan. Dan scowled. Connor looked like a little kid trapped between warring parents.

Ryan shook his head, but Connor followed Dan toward Nathan's table. They sat down beside him, one on either side.

Mr. Chen was a couple of tables away, watching and sipping his coffee.

Shit, it's going down, thought Ryan. *Stay out of it. You'll be out soon. Not your problem.*

Nathan kept eating in silence. The three guys finished at the same time. Nathan got up and started walking toward the garbage disposal. Connor stood up. Tray in hand, he followed Nathan. As he neared Nathan, he raised the tray, preparing to strike Nathan's head.

Then the tray came down with a thunderous crash on a table.

Nathan spun, his fists up and ready.

"No!" Connor yelled at Dan.

"No one says no to me," Dan screamed. He jumped up. His chair crashed to the floor. Connor stood still. His face was pale.

Dan lunged toward Connor. Mr. Chen

sprang into action wedging himself between them. Dan's fist connected with Mr. Chen's face. Mr. Chen crashed to the ground, blood dripping from his nose. His black-rimmed glasses shattered on the floor.

"You bastard," Dan yelled and hurled himself at Mr. Chen.

Ryan leapt from his chair, hopped over the table, and tackled Dan from behind. The two crashed to the floor next to Mr. Chen. Heavy punches flew as Ryan and Dan pounded each other. Mr. Chen pressed the alarm button on his spider.

Guards rushed in the room yelling. Strong hands grabbed Ryan. He didn't resist. Two guards wrestled Dan as he swore, kicked, and bit.

Ryan turned to see who held him. It was Mr. Abbot. His grip was like a vice. Ryan was hauled out of the eating area and down the hall. He knew where he was going. Solitary.

Chapter 21

Solitary

"Well, Mr. Jenkins, you've done it now," said Mr. Abbot. He put Ryan in a small beige cell. "You'll be here briefly, then it's adult prison for you, mister. You'll be there till kingdom come. Lucky I arrived, or I'd have missed the pleasure of seeing you where you belong."

He slammed the clear-plastic door shut, leaving Ryan standing next to a cot and a toilet with no lid. Ryan's legs gave way, and he sat on the edge of the cot. He put his head in his hands and stared at the cell floor.

He heard Dan and two guards enter the solitary unit.

"I'll get you for this, you bastard," Dan yelled, as he passed Ryan's cell.

"Shut up, Mr. Main," said one of the guards as they put him in the cell two down from Ryan's. But Dan wouldn't shut up. He continued to scream, yell, and bang on the walls of the small cell.

"I'm an idiot," muttered Ryan. "All I had to do was sit there and do nothing, and I ruined it." But somewhere deep inside, he knew he couldn't have just watched.

Now I'll never get out of this place, Ryan thought. *The plans, school, a job, a place of my own. Who was I kidding? Just a lot of disappointment. Nothing ever turns out right. It's over.*

It was the worst twenty-four hours of his life. Ryan's mind spun in black circles, everything swirling downward into a bottomless pit. Life didn't seem worth it. He tried to think of Pete and the road trip, but that made it worse. There was no way out, no hope, just darkness in an endless night.

In the morning, Mr. Abbot came for Ryan. His eye was twitching. "The warden wants to see you," he said, unlocking the door.

Ryan sat up. His feet hit the ground beside his cot, and he shoved them into his shoes. His whole body ached. He stunk of sweat. He stepped out of the small room. Escorted by Mr. Abbot, Ryan walked to the warden's office.

As he entered the office, Ryan was surprised to see Mr. Chen. The guard's nose was bandaged, and his eyes looked like a raccoon's.

The warden, a short man, sat behind an oversized desk. He asked Ryan to sit down. "Mr. Chen saw me early this morning," the warden said. "He went to the hospital after yesterday's incident, and I was off sick. Neither of us knew you were in solitary. If I had known, it wouldn't have happened. You stopped Mr. Chen from getting hurt further and allowed him to call for back up."

Ryan was surprised by what he was hearing. His mouth couldn't move, so he nodded.

"You'll be moving to another pod," said the warden.

"Thank you, sir."

Ryan stood up and left with Mr. Chen. As they walked down the hall, Mr. Chen stopped. "I'd like to thank you, Ryan," he said. "If there is anything I can do when you get out — an ear to listen, or whatever — please let me know."

"Thanks."

"Are you okay, Ryan?"

"Yeah, I'm fine." Ryan suddenly realized that he believed it.

When they arrived at the new pod, Nathan and Connor had already moved in. Ryan joined them for a breakfast of pancakes and bacon.

"Good to see you guys," Ryan said. "How did you get here?"

"Mr. Abbot wanted to know what went on," explained Connor. "We told him. Then he moved us." Connor smiled. "Thanks for helping me stand up to Dan."

"That goes double for me," said Nathan.

Ryan smiled. "Man, this food tastes good," he said.

"Yeah," said Connor. "Best meal I've tasted in a long time."

Nathan nodded and smiled. It was the first time Ryan had seen Nathan smile.

Ryan thought about how scared he had been in solitary. He wondered how he would have felt if he hadn't helped Nathan, Connor, and Mr. Chen. The word, "lousy" popped into his mind.

With Dan out of his life, Ryan figured there would be peace in the pod. It would not be long until Christmas. And on New Year's Day he'd be out.

Ryan studied and wrote his final math exam. While waiting for the results, he worked with Connor and saw Raj.

Raj helped Ryan with his job searches, discussed life skills, and advised him on how to find a place to stay. Ryan had applied for housing through social services and had an interview with the youth housing society, but he hadn't heard back from either.

As he entered the classroom on December 11, Ms. Standish smiled at him and said, "Mr. Jenkins, please come to the front of the room."

Ryan walked forward and stood beside the teacher.

"I am very pleased, Mr. Jenkins, to announce that you have graduated." She handed Ryan a rolled-up certificate with a ribbon around it. Everyone clapped. "This is a well-earned graduation. Something you can be very proud about."

Ms. Standish shook his hand and turned to the rest of the students. "I believe every one of you can earn this certificate. You can do it. I know you can, and Mr. Jenkins is proof of that." Ms. Standish smiled at Ryan. "Do you have anything you'd like to say?"

A huge smile crossed Ryan's face. He threw the certificate up in the air and yelled, "Finally, Yahoo!"

The students laughed and hooted.

Ryan was still smiling when he went to bed that night. He didn't care that there was no grad dance, hugs, or photographs. It didn't matter. He was congratulating himself.

The next morning, Ryan sat with Connor and Nathan as they ate their cereal. He still felt pumped. It was such a high. He couldn't remember the last time he'd felt this good.

Chapter 22

Holidays

The day after Ryan's graduation, juvie started getting ready for Christmas. Everyone was involved. At breakfast, Mr. Chen approached Ryan, Connor, and Nathan. He asked if they would like to join a few kids and a couple of guards on a trip to find a tree in the forest.

A chance to get out, even for a day? Ryan thought. *I'll take it. Even if it is for Christmas.*

The tree hunting day was perfect. As they walked back to juvie, Mr. Chen chatted to Ryan and the guys. "That tree you chose for the gym is great. But I'll need some help decorating it. Would you guys like to help?"

Connor and Nathan nodded.

Ryan shook his head. "Christmas is just a lot of disappointment. Count me out."

"I hear you," said Mr. Chen. "But helping out might be fun. A lot of guys here have never had a real Christmas. We try our best to give them one."

Ryan hesitated. Then he said, "All right. I'll help."

The huge tree looked good in the gym. Everyone helped light it and place the ornaments on the branches. Ryan didn't tell anyone he really liked the tree. His dad had never brought one home.

✳ ✳ ✳

Ryan's job search kept him busy. He'd almost forgotten about the housing applications. He was surprised and anxious when Mr. Chen asked him to come with him to see Raj.

"I have some good news and some not-so good news," said Raj. "The housing society has put you on a wait list. You may get a place before you're nineteen. You can stay there until you finish school, get a job, and are settled."

Ryan smiled. It was the best news he'd heard.

Raj's face turned serious. "Ryan, your probation officer may not hear from social services about housing until late January. But you still need a place to stay when you get out."

"That's okay," said Ryan. "I have enough money for one month's rent. I could get a room at the YMCA or bunk with some people I know. I put in job applications for the mill and other places. I may get lucky. If I can survive the winter, then in the spring I'll plant tree seedlings for a logging company, or fight forest fires. It's hard work but decent money."

"It sounds like a good plan. Your luck is changing," said Raj.

As he left the counselling office, Ryan realized he had made his own luck. The thought made him smile.

His mood changed when he got to his classroom. He found Ms. Standish and some of the guys practising holiday songs for the Christmas show. Ryan shook his head. "Christmas," he muttered. "I wish it was over."

Ms. Standish was all into the holiday. With her help, some of the students had come up with skits for the show. Others had joined the choir.

Somehow, Ms. Standish talked Ryan into helping Nathan and Connor make sets. He was surprised to find how much he enjoyed painting backdrops.

On the day before Christmas, the show was held in the gym. Connor, Ryan, Nathan, and a few other guys sat in the audience with Mr. Chen and Raj. Ryan couldn't help himself as he laughed at the skits. As he sang along with the choir, he looked over at Connor,

Nathan, Mr. Chen, and Raj. They were singing "We Wish You a Merry Christmas." *Maybe*, he thought, *being with people you care for is what Christmas is all about.*

After the show, small presents and candy were passed out, compliments of juvie. Guys who had families visited with them in the family room. Ryan and Connor went with some of the other guys to their pod.

Connor's shoulders slouched as he sat next to Ryan. "It sucks," he said.

"What sucks?" asked Ryan.

"Nathan's getting a present from his family, but I don't even know where my family is. I've been living with foster families for years. Can't remember the last time I got a present from someone who gave a damn about me."

Ryan put his hand in his pocket. He pulled something out and placed it on the table.

Connor looked down at a small carving of a bear.

"This is for you," said Ryan. "I finished it.

It turned out good, and I wanted you to have it. I couldn't have done it without you."

Tears appeared in Connor's eyes. He wiped them away with the back of his hand. "That's the best present I ever had. Thanks, Ryan."

Ryan felt choked up inside. He figured giving a gift was a double present — one you gave to a person you cared about, and one you gave yourself by making them happy.

The big Christmas dinner was lip-smacking good. *Being with friends made it taste even better*, Ryan thought.

That night Ryan lay on his bed mulling over Christmas. He smiled as he remembered the skits, the choir, Connor's gift, and the turkey drumstick. Most of all he thought about the people in his life. For the first time, he had really enjoyed Christmas.

He couldn't help thinking about Pete. What was Christmas like for him? Was he out of the hospital? Then Ryan remembered that he'd probably never see Pete again. Even if he was back on the road, he was probably mad at Ryan for not telling him about his CSO.

"Get on with your life," he muttered to himself. "You've got good things ahead." He repeated those words for the next six days, trying to make the memories of his friend fade.

***

Ryan dressed and made his bed. He joined Connor and Nathan as they left their bedrooms. Ryan looked at the calendar stuck to the pod's wall. December 31. The next day he'd be free of juvie.

"Boy, I can't wait to get out of here," Ryan said.

"You're one lucky dude," said Connor as they ate their breakfasts. Connor sounded happy, but Ryan thought his face had a hangdog look.

"Don't worry," said Ryan. "Nathan is here. And when I can, I'll come and see you."

"You will?"

"If I can't see you, I'll write."

"Wow. I've never gotten a letter from anyone."

"Well, mine will be the first. When I get a job, I can pay for a phone. Maybe you can earn some money when you get out and buy one too. I can message you. Just don't steal a cell, okay? You don't need to be back in here."

"What are you going to do, Ryan?" asked Nathan.

Ryan explained his plan, then added. "I've booked a room at the YMCA. I'll work for a year, then go to school. No sweat." He made himself sound confident. But he was worried. He wished there was someone there for him if the going got tough.

"Yeah," said Connor. "No sweat."

Chapter 23

Arrival

That night, Ryan sat in the common eating area enjoying a dinner of turkey pot pie. He chatted with Connor and Nathan.

He flinched as Mr. Abbot stepped in front of him.

"Mr. Jenkins, come with me. Someone wants to see you."

Ryan followed Mr. Abbot out of the eating area and into the concrete halls. His mind whirled like a Vegas slot machine trying to catch the right combination.

It isn't a regular visitors' day — wrong day and wrong time, he thought. *Besides, who the hell ever visits me?*

It had to be trouble for sure — the warden, his probation officer. Ryan's mind continued to spin until it came to a jerky stop on the worst scenario: the warden. But why? Beads of sweat ran down his back. His neck was stiff. He hardly noticed where they were walking.

Then Mr. Abbot stopped. Ryan looked up and his eyes widened. The guard at the entrance to the visitors' room opened the glass-windowed door.

Ryan stepped inside. A man, sitting with his back to him, rose and turned.

The mask of worry Ryan wore fell apart into a smile. "Pete, my God, you're okay. I thought I'd never see you again. You came back. No one ever comes back." The words spilled out before Ryan could stop them.

"I did. I came back. You saved my life.

You're my bro. We watch out for each other."
Pete's grin was wide.

Ryan felt his face heat up as he stared at
the truck driver in the leather jacket. Pete was
standing there with his hands in his pockets
and a half-smile on his face.

"Come on, sit down by the window,
invited Pete. "Take a load off your feet." He
beckoned toward the chairs.

Ryan's legs were on autopilot and obeyed.
He sat beside Pete.

They talked about the accident and its
aftermath. Pete told Ryan about his recovery.
"The doctor gave me the go-ahead a few weeks
ago. I've been hauling freight since then. I
lined up a load to haul here. I thought I'd see
how you're doing. I saw the warden and your
probation officer this afternoon. They tell me
you're getting out tomorrow. The warden said
you get a farewell and the clothes you arrived
in. What's your plan?"

Ryan grinned. For once he had an answer

to that question. "For sure school when I'm nineteen. But for now, I booked a room at the YMCA, and I have an interview for a job next week. If I get it, that will help with rent. That's it, I guess."

"How's a seat in a semi sound?" asked Pete. "I've been looking for a swamper to help on the long hauls across Canada. You can still get your education. We'll work it out. If you want, I'll help you get your licence to drive a semi. If you decide to join me, the warden and your probation officer told me what I need to do."

Ryan couldn't speak. He stared out the window, but he found that the view was blurry. A tear stung his eye, and he wiped it away with the back of his sleeve. "Damn allergies," he said.

Pete looked at the floor. "Yeah," he said, "Bad time of year. They've been bothering me too." Then he looked up with a grin. "Snow does that. So what is it, yes or no?"

"Yes," said Ryan. "Hell, yes."

Acknowledgements

There is always a hidden story behind each page of a book. That story is the author's journey while creating the book. I have been fortunate to have people with me on that journey who have supported and guided me. I would like to thank those who have enabled me to write my stories.

To my family: Dennis for your friendship, love, honesty, and patience. Sean, Kelly Anne, Jackie, and Kelly Lee for supporting my endeavours. To my grandsons Thorin and Lennox — you make me smile.

For your friendship, support and wisdom, I wish to thank the members of the writing groups I belong to especially: Sylvia Sikundar, Allison Douglas-Tourner, Delia McCrae, Renee Miller, Catherine Pledger, Annely So, Moira Gardner, and a special thank you to Anne Patton for going above and beyond.

To Leanne Jones, David and Lenore

Thomas — your thoughtful comments made the book better.

To my mentor Cathleen With, instructor Claire Mulligan, and James Lorimer and Company editor Kat Mototsune for their guidance and furthering my knowledge.